Long John

William Henry John was a small-time rancher. But when his wife died in a riding accident, he became a broken man.

He turned to drink.

At first his neighbours were helpful and sympathetic, but Henry John soon became the town drunk and ignored by all.

Then one day his life changed. He saved the life of a young woman whom he thought was his dead wife. She thanked him and gave him a kiss on the cheek.

From that day forth, William Henry John became a changed, if disturbed man.

By the same author

Woebegone
Last Stop Liberty
Death Storm
Burnout!
Deadly Venom
Blood Money

As Adam Smith
Stolen Fortunes
Money Thicker Than
Blood

As Will Black
Avengers from Hell
Tombstone Scarlet
The Legend of Broken
Saddle
Death Comes Easy
Blood River
Whiteout!

As Jay D. West
Sharper
Sharper: Avenging Gun
Angel of Death: Sharper
Sharper's Revenge
Sharper's Quest

As Del R. Doyle
Showdown in Ghost
Creek
Blood at Ghost Creek
Rustlers at Ghost Creek
Ghost Creek Renegades

As Ben Ray
Yellow Streak
Gunslingers
The Plains Killers
A Rolling Stone
Badge of Office

Long John

D.D. Lang

A Black Horse Western

ROBERT HALE

© D.D. Lang 2018
First published in Great Britain 2018

ISBN 978-0-7198-2628-3

The Crowood Press
The Stable Block
Crowood Lane
Ramsbury
Marlborough
Wiltshire SN8 2HR

www.bhwesterns.com

Robert Hale is an imprint
of The Crowood Press

Typeset by
Derek Doyle & Associates, Shaw Heath
Printed and bound in Great Britain by
CPI Group (UK) Ltd, Croydon, CR0 4YY

To Leah, my daughter,
whose help was greatly appreciated

PROLOGUE

The Wells Fargo stagecoach pulled into the stage depot, the driver slumped forward, then fell ten feet to the ground.

The shotgun rider was missing. The rear of the coach was peppered with arrows. It was a miracle he'd escaped the Indian war party at all, let alone as a survivor.

A tall, lean man got out of the passenger compartment and looked down at the fallen man. The driver was dead, he knew that. The driver's sightless, brown eyes stared up at the dark-clad passenger with a look of complete surprise. His mouth was open, and from one corner a trickle of blood meandered down his chin and plop-plopped into the dust. His shirt front was soaked in blood, as was his back.

There were no other passengers. The man clambered aboard the stagecoach for the last time and grabbed the handles of his carpetbag and, without a word or backward glance, strode off into town.

Questions by the stage depot manager were fired at him as he left, but the man didn't even turn around to acknowledge them, so the manager went for the sheriff.

The tall man made an imposing picture. At least six-foot five inches in his stockinged feet, he walked down the centre of Main Street. Dressed in a black jacket with matching trousers and Stetson, his white shirt was pristine as if he'd just put it on. The boot-lace tie round his neck bore a silver bull's head, his waistcoat, a bright-red satin. The boots, of the best quality and highly polished.

A scar ran down the left side of his face and curved under his nose, hidden by a large, black moustache that was neatly trimmed. His sideburns were long and equally black.

Piercing, dark-brown eyes stared neither to the left, nor the right as he sought his destination.

The hotel, like all small-town hotels, was next door to the saloon. Probably owned by the same man, he thought, as he climbed the wooden steps that led onto the boardwalk.

The town was relatively quiet at this time of the day, four in the afternoon. He checked his watch and put it back in his waistcoat pocket. He painted the very image of a Mississippi gambler, except for his guns.

Strapped to both thighs were a pair of silver and pearl Colts, hung low, gunslinger-style. The handles reflected the late afternoon sun as he stood on the boardwalk and surveyed the town.

Medicine Head was indeed a small town. One street, Main Street, ran from east to west, on either side stood single storey buildings, wooden, except for the bank and the sheriff's office.

He looked up at the hotel. It was the only two-storeyed building in town. Symmetrical in design, a wide, double-door entrance, and three windows on either side. The first floor had a balcony that ran all the way around; it was empty.

Opposite the hotel was a general store, closed. Next to that the bank and the sheriff's office.

On this side of the street, the saloon and various private houses lined what was left of the main street.

The livery stable was next to the bank and he crossed the street.

A huge, black man was hammering away with a large hammer in his right hand. In his left, a large pair of tongs held a red-hot horseshoe he was aiming to fix to the bay in the stall.

The tall man looked in the stable and saw several horses, turned, and without saying a word, he re-crossed the street to the hotel. Dan Briggs, the livery owner cum blacksmith, watched as he crossed the street, the huge hammer in mid-air.

The tall man looked around over his shoulder, he eyed Dan and turned back again. The hammer came down on the shoe.

Entering the hotel, he walked to the desk and hit the bell.

Nobody answered.

He hit the bell again. From the office at the rear he could hear movement, papers being shuffled, a chair knocked over. Whoever was in there had obviously been asleep.

The door opened and an old man, well into his sixties, wearing a grimy-grey vest that had once been white, dishevelled hair and two day's stubble, emerged.

'Yeah?'

'Room.'

'You want one?'

The tall man just stared. His sharp, deep eyes obviated the need for the old man to ask further questions.

'Sign here,' the desk clerk pointed at the register.

The tall men picked up the pen and wrote a name. 'Welcome, Mr— hell, I can't read your writin'.'

The tall man picked up the key to his room and climbed the stairs.

The room was as he would have expected. A

single bed in one corner with a small table to the side with an old oil-lamp. A chest of four drawers, with a jug and washbowl on top against one wall, a large window in another, and a tallboy and a rickety wooden chair completed the furnishings. The ceiling might well have been white once, now it was stained by tobacco smoke and matched the drab colour of the walls.

Throwing his saddle-bags on the bed, he took his Stetson off and hung it on the back of the chair. The jug was full of water so he emptied some into the bowl and splashed his face. Even though the water was tepid, he felt better.

Pouring some water into his hand, he swilled the inside of his mouth, trying to get the dust out and spat into the bowl.

He took a wooden comb from his inside pocket and ran it through his thick, black hair, replaced his Stetson and left the room. The saloon was his next port of call.

The wind had begun to pick up again, dust blew and settled on everything. The yellow clouds swirled and at times had been known to block out the sunlight.

The street was deserted. Opposite the saloon, a flat-back with a four-team stood impatiently pawing at the ground, their cargo of straw bales being attacked by the wind and sand sending wisps into the air.

There were only a dozen people in the saloon. The bat-wing doors squeaked as he pushed them open. As usual, most people in the saloon turned as he entered. When they saw it was a stranger, nobody made eye contact. It was the sort of situation he'd been in many times before. If the piano player had been playing – he would have stopped – adding more atmosphere.

He walked up to the bar and threw down a dime. 'Whiskey.'

The barkeep brought a bottle up from beneath the counter, the silver pouring spout caught the light as he tilted it into a one-shot glass, filling it to the brim.

The tall man picked the glass up, held it up to the light, to check there was nothing in there he hadn't paid for, and, bringing it to his lips, knocked it back in one.

Slamming the glass back on the counter, indicating he wanted it filled, he took out a silver cigar case from the inside pocket of his jacket. Opening it, he took out a long, narrow cigar and placed it between thin lips. He closed the case and returned it to the pocket.

The barkeep struck a match. The man, without raising his head, looked the barkeep full in the eye. Then he leant forward and drew on the cigar, blowing out a cloud of blue-grey smoke.

'Thanks.'

The barkeep nodded and filled the glass. This time, he left the bottle on the counter, then took out a cloth and went through the time-honoured barkeep job of wiping down an already clean bartop. It was more habit than necessity.

Downing his second glassful, he picked up the bottle, looked at the label – it was a brand he'd never heard of – and poured another glass.

After the fifth drink, he relaxed some. He began to look around the saloon. The room was square and the bar filled up one entire wall. There was a full-length mirror behind it which had seen better days, but it managed to make the saloon look far bigger than it actually was.

With his back to the bar, the bat-wing doors were in front of him, to his left a blank wall. No window, or pictures broke up the monotony of the plain, brown, painted surface.

To his right, a staircase swept from the wooden floor up to a landing which disappeared back over the bar.

The tables, old and rickety, were circular. Covered in stain rings from whiskey and beer, the edges marked where cigars or cigarettes had burned.

At the table nearest the staircase sat four cowboys. They were playing poker quietly. Between the staircase and the bar, another game was in progress, this one was noisier; it was obvious the participants had had a lot to drink.

A hand was won and a flurry of activity took place as the man with his back to the bar began to pull the nickels and dimes and dollar bills that were his prize, towards him.

It looked as if the winner hadn't won in a long time. Judging by the way he tried to stand, he'd been drinking longer than he'd been playing.

Drunkenly, the man staggered towards the bar intent on buying a round of drinks. His sense of balance was only matched by his clumsiness. Turning towards his card-playing friends, he backed into the tall man.

Not content with knocking the stranger's drink all down his vest, in an effort to make things better, he only made them worse. As he tried to dry the man off, losing his balance completely, he fell straight into him almost taking him down.

The tall man stood his ground and stared with disgust at the fallen man.

'Hell, give me a hand here,' the man said.

The tall stranger merely turned his back on him, willing to let things be.

This was not good enough for the drunkard.

Scrambling to his feet he stood wavering. 'I asked you fer a hand, stranger, what's the matter wi' you?'

'Let it go, friend,' the stranger replied.

'Hell no. I ain't letting it go,' the man said, bracing himself on the bar.

In the meantime, his card-playing friends were calling him back, telling him to forget it.

'Now you damn well apologize, mister,' the drunk said.

The tall stranger ignored him again.

'I said—'

'I heard what you said, boy, now listen to me. Let it be.'

'You chicken-shit yeller, or what?'

The saloon went deathly quiet. This was an insult that had to be answered.

The tall man placed his empty whiskey glass back on the bar and turned around to face his antagonist.

'Say what?' he said.

The man was too drunk to be afraid. 'I said, mister high-an'-mighty, you chicken-shit yeller!'

'That's what I thought you said, mister. Now, you're drunk, and I'm sober, so why don't you go back over to your friends and play cards?'

The drunkard laughed. 'See that boys? The man's chicken-shit yeller. I bet ya his momma was a whore, too,' and he continued laughing. He was the only one in the saloon who was.

Reluctantly, the tall man turned for the final time. This last insult, drunk or no, could not be ignored.

Opening his jacket, revealing his twin pistols, he stood feet apart, arms hanging loosely at his sides.

'This what you want, boy?' he said.

Letting go of the bar, the drunk man swayed as he tried to imitate the stance. 'Ready when you are, chicken-shit.'

Those were his last words.

The drunkard drew surprisingly quickly, but not quickly enough.

Even as he cocked the hammer of his Colt and loosed off a shot, the tall man had drawn and fired. There was no mistaking the action of a gunslinger.

The drunkard stood stock-still. Eyes wide open in disbelief, all signs of his four hours drinking disappeared as he looked down at the hole in his chest.

He looked up at the tall man, then slowly fell over backwards, his gun clattering to the wooden floor.

The saloon was deathly quiet. No one dared speak or move in case they became the next victim.

The stranger cast his eyes around the saloon, just in case the man's friends tried to take him on. He saw the looks in their eyes and knew it was safe enough to re-holster his weapon.

Turning back to his bottle, he filled the glass one more time and sank the burning liquid.

The bat-wing doors flew open and Sheriff Luke McCabe, rifle at the ready, stood in the doorway, staring into the saloon.

16

'What's goin' on in here?' he asked no one in particular.

Silence greeted his question.

He stared from face to face, each man avoiding his gaze.

'I ain't askin' agen,' he said and loaded the rifle.

The barkeep, who'd been hiding behind the bar, raised his head and peered over the counter.

'Clem was drunk, Sheriff,' he said. 'He wouldn't shut his big mouth. This fella here, had no choice.'

'That true?' the sheriff asked the room.

He was greeted by nods and grunts – albeit grudgingly.

Luke McCabe walked up to the stranger. 'I don't like trouble in my town,' he said.

'Me neither,' the man answered.

'You plannin' on stayin'?'

'Nope.'

'Good.'

The sheriff stared at the stranger for a few long seconds and then, without turning his head or taking his eyes off the man, he called out for someone to get the undertaker.

'You better get Sadie, too,' he added.

'If I were you,' the sheriff went on, 'I'd drink up an' hightail it afore his wife gets here.'

'Sheriff, I ain't committed no crime. I shot in self-defence.'

' 'Tis a piece o' friendly advice is all,' the sheriff said and added, 'I wanna see you afore you go. Need some answers 'bout the stagecoach.'

'I'll see you later, Sheriff.'

The tall man continued to drink his whiskey. Nearly half the bottle had disappeared, but it didn't seem to have the slightest effect on him.

He'd just downed another glass when the bat-wing doors were flung back with such force they hit the walls on either side.

'Where's the bastard who killed my Clem?' a woman screamed at the top of her voice.

Again, the saloon went quiet. All eyes went from Sadie Webster to the tall stranger.

She didn't need to ask again.

Walking up to within five feet of him she called out, 'Mister!'

The stranger turned just as both barrels of the shotgun went off.

CHAPTER ONE

The bright sunlight shone straight in the man's face
through the hole in the dusty curtain. Covering his
eyes, he groaned.

Another day.

The homestead was getting the better of him.
Since the death of his wife in a riding accident, the
work-load was more than he could manage with a
perpetual hangover.

Neighbours had been sympathetic and helpful –
at first – but they had their own spreads to run, their
own mouths to feed. As soon as he hit the bottle,
they hit the road.

The drinking had become a part of life now, from
breakfast onwards, he was never without a bottle.

Once a month he'd go into town for provisions,
get blind-drunk in the saloon and spend the night
in the buckboard. The townsfolk began to ignore

him. There was a limit to their tolerance. In their eyes, mourning was over – life began.

To William Henry John, however, his life was over. From being a hard-working, loving husband, he'd degenerated into the once-a-month town drunk he now was. It seemed that nothing would change that. Until one fateful morning.

Henry John was just waking up in the back of the buckboard. He'd spent the cold night beneath a tarpaulin and was still hungover and sore.

He sat up – just – and peered around with a dazed, bleary, expression of someone who, not only didn't know where they were, but didn't even know who he was.

He rubbed his eyes and yawned, the effort sent a pang of pain running from behind both eyes down to his boots. He held his head.

The everyday sounds of the town assailed his ears like a herd of buffalo stampeding across broken glass.

For the hundredth time in his short life, he vowed never to touch a drop again. And he sat and he sat until he felt he could move without cracking open like an egg.

People passed his buckboard without giving him a second glance, he ignored them also. He stared at the empty buckboard, wondering what it was he should have in it. Then he remembered. Provisions.

Reaching into his back pocket, he pulled out an old, leather wallet and readied himself to get to the hardware-cum-grocery store.

Fumbling with fingers that didn't seem to want to work in anything remotely resembling a coordinated movement, he unfolded the wallet and peered inside.

It was empty.

Shit! he thought, *I been robbed.*

Then he remembered the saloon. He'd done it again.

Throwing the wallet to the ground, he stood up, wavered and plonked back down again – hard.

This seemed to shock some of the lethargy out of him and he stood again.

This time he swayed some, but didn't fall over.

The pair, who'd been hitched to the wagon all night, looked to be in an equally bad way. He thought about unhitching them and giving them some food and water, but he doubted whether he could manage that just now. The best thing, he thought, was to drive the buckboard to the trough and park it end-on so they could drink, then he'd throw a feed bag over them so they could eat. Satisfied with his plan, forgetting that this was what he did every month, he climbed onto the driving seat and untied the reins.

The horses needed no prompting. Lazily they

walked across Main to the livery stable and straight to the water trough. Henry John felt pleased with himself that he'd managed to complete the task.

Next, he picked up the two feed bags and waited until the horses had finished drinking, then he placed the bags over the horses' heads and climbed back on the buckboard.

He folded the tarpaulin as neatly as he could and then yawned and stretched. It was a long fifteen miles back to the homestead. It would be an even longer month with no food and no money, but he'd get by; he always did.

Further along Main Street, gunfire broke out; three rapid shots followed by silence. Henry John tried to see where it was coming from. He couldn't.

He could, however, hear hoofbeats and the high-pitched scream of a woman. From out of an alleyway, a one-horse trap careened into Main and headed straight towards Henry John's wagon.

For a second or two he just stood and stared. The young woman in the trap had the reins tied round one wrist and she fought to free herself. The gunfire had bolted the horse. It was out of control.

In that instant, William Henry John was sober. Riding towards him was his dead wife. It was happening all over again, but this time he'd do something about it.

Never taking his eyes from the trap, he moved to

the back of the buckboard and waited. He prayed that the horse would not swerve out of his reach, and that his own animals didn't shift.

Closer and closer the trap came. The townsfolk stood with mouths open, not one of them moved. The woman's screams and shouts for help went almost unheeded. Almost, but not quite.

John Henry steadied himself. All thoughts of headache and sickness vanished, he was about to save the life of his dead wife. This time he'd do it. This time she'd be safe.

As the trap approached, he poised himself, preparing to leap.

At exactly the right moment, he leapt. The speed of the trap carried him forward, he managed to hold on with one hand, and one of his feet felt as if it could take his weight.

Hanging on for dear life, he battled his way into the trap. The woman had ceased screaming, but Henry John took no notice of her, his eyes on the reins, the horse, and most of all, the large wheel that was right behind him, waiting to cut him in two if he fell.

It seemed that his arms would be pulled from their sockets as he fought gravity trying to force his way into the trap and free the reins. The horse, still scared out of its wits, was bolting hell for leather. The animal's ears were pinned back and every now and then, Henry John saw the whites of the frightened animal's eyes and caught flecks of foam in his face and hair.

William Henry John was a big man, but a big man who was seriously out of condition. It took him five hard, long minutes to get inside the trap, he was wheezing so much he could hardly breathe. No sooner had he breathed in than his body forced the air out again, never giving him enough time to catch his breath.

He managed to free the reins from the woman's wrist and he slowly reined the animal to a halt.

No sooner had the horse come to a panting halt, Henry John felt the throbbing in his head; the headache was back, if indeed, it had ever left.

The woman threw her arms around his neck and kissed him gently on the cheek. She could smell the sourness of his whiskey-soaked breath. She could smell the staleness of his body and, worst of all, the stench of dried vomit which littered his vest, shirt and breeches.

She took her arms from his neck and primly placed them in her own lap, eyes downcast.

'I don't know who you are,' she said, softly, 'but I owe you my life.'

William Henry John was still finding it difficult to get his breath, the air kept escaping, he couldn't understand why.

'Hell ma'am – 'scuse me, ma'am – 'tweren't nothin',' he managed to say.

'It may be nothing to you, Mister—?'

'John, William Henry John,' he gasped.

'Mr John. It may be nothing to you, but I kinda like my life. I'm very grateful. Is there anything I can do for you?'

'Ain't no need, ma'am,' he wheezed.

'Please, I'd like to do something.'

William Henry John was beginning to panic a little. His breath was coming in short pants, he'd black out soon if it didn't stop.

'You could drive me – back to – the livery – stable,' he said.

'A pleasure, Mr John.'

She took the reins from his limp hands and turned the buggy around.

'Please, if there's anything I can do—'

Henry John shook his head, he couldn't get enough air to speak.

Clambering on to his own buckboard, he picked up the reins and buffalo-hide whip and drove his team out of town.

He was vaguely aware of cheering, and clapping and people calling out his name, but he took no notice, no one ever spoke to him anymore. *I must be hallucinating*, he thought.

Back home, he unhitched the horses and led

them to the corral. He didn't have the energy to get to the house, so he flopped down in the barn and slept.

He was being carried.

He could feel the fingers digging into his armpits, felt them also around his ankles. Opening his eyes, he closed them again immediately. The sun was directly overhead.

He tried once again to open his eyes. Screwing up his face, he squinted, but all he could see were the black silhouettes of the two men that had his legs. The one whose fingers were beginning to hurt his armpits was just a blur.

He felt the three men begin to climb steps and he heard their leather soles as they hit the wooden boards.

Then it was darker. He could sense that without opening his eyes. He didn't want to open them anyway, they felt better closed.

He felt the softness of the bed as he was lowered, his breathing became easier, not perfect, just easier. He thought about opening his eyes, but decided against it, then slept.

He was at his wife's funeral. The whole town was there, she is – was – a beautiful woman. Long, black hair, thicker than a horse's mane. The most piercing grey eyes he'd ever seen set either side of a perfect nose above ruby-red lips that were made for kissing.

The coffin was lowered into the ground and he wondered who was in it.

He'd have to pull himself together, he thought. He'd start right now. No more booze. Get the homestead back and running. Got to make some money. Maybe sell up and ride. Nothing to stay here for.

So, it was gone. The house, the corral, the barn, the land. He sold it all.

The desert was a hot, lonely place. Sand dunes as far as the eye could see, which was not far. He'd hoped for a different view when he crested each dune, but the view was the same.

He rode all day, he felt nothing. At nightfall, he made camp and lit a fire. Coffee on, bacon sizzling, the air cooling. He ate. His breath was coming in those short, raspy pants again, he couldn't understand why. He slept.

The next day was like the last, and the next, and the next. Nothing changed. Was he riding around in circles?

He saw the green in the distance. Or was it a hallucination? What did they call it? Mirage. Yes, that was it. Was it a mirage? He'd soon find out.

The heat haze made everything shimmer. There were no defined edges to anything. Even his horse's head shimmered in front of him. The green stayed where it was.

He rode on, he wasn't thinking about anything. He concentrated on the green.

It got closer. He could make out the glistening shapes of giant cactus and trees. They were there. It wasn't a mirage. The sand gave way to rocky ground which gave way to patchy grassland and scrub. There was smoke ahead.

Riding tall in the saddle, he entered town. Was it another town, or the same one? They all began to look the same. The clapboard fronts, the sidewalks, the saloons, the hotels. A store here and there, a livery stable, a blacksmith, some houses. The jail.

He checked into the hotel, then took a bath and shave from the barber shop across the street. He felt a new man. He looked a new man.

The café was on the corner, next to the bank. The smell of food drew him there. He realized he was hungry.

The town was apparently called Lucklaw and was just inside the state of Arizona. He'd happened there by chance, but then he'd happened everywhere by chance.

The town had sprung up as a cattle-feed station some fifteen years earlier. Mushrooming in the early days, it had now settled down to stagnate gently. Life was reasonable, the law was upheld and everyone was happy.

William Henry John finished his meal, drank his coffee and walked back to the hotel. Maybe he'd stay here for a while, get a job, see what was on offer.

It didn't take him long. The livery-manager had broken his leg and would be off work for at least eight to ten weeks. Henry John got the job. It wasn't too taxing. Grooming, cleaning out the stalls, feeding and banking the money as and when it came in.

Perhaps manager was too grand a description, as he was the only employee; whenever anything needed doing, William Henry John did it.

Life was good. His room and board at the hotel was comfortable, his horse was stabled and fed for free, and he made a lot of friends. Pretty soon, he was popular with almost everyone.

It seemed he'd found the ideal place to spend at least the next phase of his life.

Dorothy Brown came on to the scene.

She was young, vivacious and had her sights on William Henry John. And to be honest, William Henry John didn't mind at all. They married and set up house together. The livery stable job became permanent, business increased as Henry John began to hire out buggies and traps as well as horses.

Children came. A boy and a girl, and for three years, William Henry John never thought about his first wife, except in his dreams.

A cattle train rolled into town. One of the biggest they'd ever seen. Consequently, there were more thirsty cowboys in town than there'd ever been in the town's short history.

It hadn't rained now for nearly six months. The river was running dry, there was talk of it drying out altogether. The cattle couldn't be moved for fear of loss.

The cowboys spent too long in town. Their money had run out, law broke down, there was simply too many men for the sheriff and the town to cope with.

Fighting was a regular occurrence and shooting became commonplace. William Henry John feared for his wife and children.

The cattle were brought closer to town so that less men were needed to keep them in check, and if something should happen that required extra manpower, well, they didn't have so far to travel.

The rains came.

With the rain came thunder and lightning and the inevitable stampede. The trail boss, a serious, experienced man, tried his best to keep the cattle out of town, but most of his men were too drunk, using up their credit at the saloon, to be of any use.

Over a thousand head of cattle ran amok through Lucklaw. Thirty-eight men, women and children were either crushed under the steers' hoofs, or flattened in their beds by their homes being knocked down in the frenetic stampede.

William Henry John lost his entire family – again.

He moved on once more, riding his old, trusty steed. His breathing was so difficult, he couldn't get enough air in.

It had been an arduous journey west; passing through Death Valley had been the worst ordeal he'd ever endured.

The air so hot it burnt your lungs as you inhaled. The temperature had been in the low hundreds for over three weeks now, and he'd only just had enough water to reach the bauxite fields.

The workers there were a mixed bunch of white men, Indians, Mexicans and Chinese. Burned so deep by the sun, their skin was almost black. These men worked shifts digging out the bauxite and loading it on to wagons for transport to Los Angeles. The journey took ten weeks and the heat was unrelenting.

Again, Henry John felt the tightness in his chest, but the cool water eased his parched throat.

He'd stayed for over a month, hoping to earn enough money to move on. The work was hard, every movement an effort. The utter desolation of the Valley was like nothing he'd ever seen before.

He'd heard stories of the Valley in the past. The

sand dunes whipped up by the winds and dumped on rocky plateaus like a pile of beans on a tin plate. The rock itself, so varied in colour it looked at times as if it'd been painted.

The bauxite fields stretched for miles. In the sunlight they shimmered, giving the impression of dark, black water.

The thirsty men had lasted from sun up to sun down and never let go. Sunstroke, sunburn and death, were commonplace.

The Chinese were the hardiest. Nothing seemed to bother them. They spoke no English and never mixed with the whites or Mexicans. They were a strange-looking people; all wore blue tunics, rarely shoes, and large, round straw hats on their heads. They never seemed to sweat, and this puzzled Henry John. But he was too hot and sweaty to bother finding out why.

To the north, the Apache war had been raging. Stories had drifted south of the slaughter that had taken place. Two of the Mexicans had been at the Camp Grant Massacre, and told of the vicious killings of Apache women and children early one morning.

Vigilantes from Tucson, led by an old Indian fighter called Oury, had taken only half an hour to 'clean up the village'. The Apaches had been asleep in bed when the attack took place, their village was fired and the women and children killed as they tried to flee.

From the little English the Mexicans spoke and the little Mexican Henry John understood, Papago mercenaries had committed the worst atrocities, even keeping some of the women and children to sell as slaves down in Mexico.

Henry John was so appalled at the stories, he feared for the very existence of the Indians.

The white men in the camp, especially when they got drunk, relived these stories, glorying in the tales and regretting the fact that they'd 'missed out' on a good Indian fight. Henry John found their behaviour sickening. Their talk of rape and murder was abhorrent to him, not that he was a great Indian lover. He'd never met any, but it just didn't seem right to him. He wondered why President Grant wasn't doing anything about it.

The conversations disgusted him and it was for that reason he decided to leave and head for the coast of California.

Henry John had heard of the great ocean, but he'd never seen it; besides, he had nothing better to do.

Getting out of Death Valley was just as bad as getting in. He spent an hour in the saddle and an hour walking as he didn't want his horse to die on him.

During the hottest part of the day, which was always between eleven and four, he rested up under whatever shade he could find. The shade kept the direct sunlight off him but not the heat. He'd sleep and dream and in his dreams, he was always in water. Cool, clear water up to his neck. The water pressure was so intense that he found it difficult to breathe, so he had to get out. Many times, he woke up bathed in sweat and, just for an instant, he believed he'd really been there. One look at the surrounding country brought him back to reality.

For three weeks, he'd not seen a soul. He could've been the last man on earth for all he knew. Then he saw the smoke.

Thick plumes of black smoke spiralled into the air. He mounted his horse and walked it to the crest of a ridge. There, spread below him, was rangeland. After so many months with no greenery, just every shade of brown imaginable, the view of the grass, no matter how sparse, was a sight to behold. He realized he'd forgotten colour.

Two miles, he reckoned, was how far away the smouldering ruins of the building lay. He couldn't see any detail, except for the stone chimney-stack that stood defiantly.

He kicked his horse on and rode down the ridge.

The building had been small, too big to be called a shack, but too small to be called a ranch-house.

The small picket fence was still standing around part of the house, behind it were flowers and vegetables. There was a dead horse, old by the look of it. The barn had also been razed.

Dismounting, he walked to theurning house. He saw the woman first.

He removed his Stetson and knelt by her side. She was naked, and her feet and the lower part of her legs were burned black by the hungry flames that had tried to devour her.

She was badly burned on the rest of her exposed skin, but this he knew was due to the sun.

Turning her over, her face made him throw up on the spot.

Her teeth had been knocked out and it looked as if her jaw was broken. One eye was completely closed and the purple-black circle had spread halfway down her cheek. The woman had been beaten.

He looked at the ground about her. There were boot prints and bits of cloth. Her clothes had obviously been ripped from her body.

By the shape of her breasts, which bore evidence of teeth marks and were spattered in blood and sand, the woman had been quite young, although it was impossible to tell how old she might have been.

Henry John lowered his head and wept. He saw his own sorrow. He cried not for this nameless woman, but for the two women he'd loved and lost. He cried for himself.

Taking out a small spade strapped to the back of his saddle, he decided the only proper thing to do was bury her and say a few words. He was not a religious man, but in his head, he had a mental picture of how the woman had died. He wasn't a tracker, but from the marks in the sand, the blood around her private parts and the finger marks on her body, he knew she'd been raped.

He dug a shallow grave and rolled the body into it. He covered her as best he could with the material that she had once worn and covered that with sand. Then he piled rocks on top of the sand and fashioned a crude cross and wedged that into the rocks. He knew it wouldn't last long but it was the best he could do.

When he'd finished, he laid the spade on the ground. He picked up his Stetson, held it in his hands, and bowed his head.

His thoughts were racing and too random for any conventional prayer to last long in his mind, and the tightness in his chest made him pant and gulp in great gulps of hot air. But no matter how deeply he inhaled, there was never enough air. Never enough.

He put his hat on and turned away from the grave. He'd done his best. He'd not inspected the rest of the small homestead. Was the woman alone?

Did her attackers take the rest? What did they want? All these questions ran through his head with the mental pictures of his own wives and children.

He walked across to the barn. There was evidence of hay and feed but nothing else. No more bodies. He was half pleased and half disappointed.

He walked around to the rear of the house and found the child.

He fell to his knees and screamed. His chest tightened, like a steel band had been wrapped around it. Having screamed, he couldn't breathe in. It was as if his lungs were trying to escape and float off into the air.

Eyes wide with terror, he collapsed head first onto the ground.

The dog licked his face. Then it licked his hand. Then it sat.

Henry John opened his eyes. He expected a coyote but what he found was a small, black mutt.

The dog's tail wagged, creating a small cloud of dust as it did so. The pink tongue lolled to the side of its panting mouth. The pin-point black eyes were bright and the ears erect with his head tilted slightly to one side. Henry John closed his eyes again. He'd been dreaming about a dead woman and a dead child. He was relieved to find it wasn't true.

Bringing his elbows up he rested on his stomach.

The tightness in his chest had gone. The air was

cooler and the night brightly lit by a full moon.

The dog stared at him with that peculiar innocence dogs portray, waiting for the man to do or say something.

Henry John threw a stone. It arced through the air for ten or twelve feet and crashed into the sand like a meteorite, leaving a small, indistinguishable crater.

The dog retracted its tongue, closed its mouth and watched the stone fly through the air.

It didn't move.

The mouth opened and the tongue lolled when the excitement was over. He returned his lop-sided gaze to the man.

Henry John rolled on to his side and sat up. His head was spinning. The large circle to his left shone a preternatural blue light that bathed the area in its glow. His hands were blue. The dog's tongue was blue.

He stood. The effort brought the pain back but he ignored it. He breathed in deeply through his nose and exhaled through his mouth. His mother had told him to do that. When?

'Breathe in through your nose and out through your mouth,' she said. 'That way, you get good, clean air in your lungs.'

He tried it again. He felt dizzy.

His horse was still where he'd left it. Munching at

the flowers and the vegetables, pawing the ground to get at the juicier roots.

He took out the coffee pot and the coffee beans. Lighting a fire, he noticed that his hands weren't blue after all. They were pink. So was the dog's tongue.

The coffee was stale. He'd had the beans for too long. It tasted bitter. Or was the taste already in his mouth? He didn't know. He drank the coffee anyway.

In the distance, a coyote or a wolf howled at the moon. The moon didn't answer. So, he picked up his spade once again and walked to the rear of the house. He wasn't dreaming. The body was still there just as it had been in his dream.

The child, a boy, maybe three or four years old, was lying on his back. Mouth open in a final scream. One eye was closed, the other wasn't there. That's where the bullet had gone in. The back of the child's head was also not there.

The body was fully clothed and he was relieved at that. Digging, his mind concentrated. Digging. He couldn't think then of anything else.

Digging.

The grave was too deep and too long. He'd dug until his arms and back and shoulders cried out to stop. The sweat, running down his face in streams. He felt cold. He stopped.

39

Straightening up, he mopped his brow with his bandanna and arched his back to relieve the strain. The band around his chest was back, so he focused on the hole again.

It was deep, bottomless and black. He was afraid he was going to fall in it. In his mind, he did. He fell, going end over end over end. But he never reached the bottom.

The dog sat and watched. He sniffed each spade-ful of sand as the hole progressed downwards and the pile progressed upwards. Nothing there for him to eat, so he waited.

Picking up the stiff, little body, Henry John placed it carefully in the hole. He expected it to drop out of sight, but it rested, gently, peacefully, on the bottom.

He began to shovel the sand back into the hole, covering the boy's head first; the eye was staring at him. In gratitude? He didn't think so. But at least the vultures wouldn't be able to rip them to shreds.

He gazed at the moon. The moon looked back and seemed to be laughing at him – or was it with him? Except, he wasn't laughing. He doubted he would laugh again.

He didn't remember falling asleep. He remem-bered the moon, and the hole, and the dog. But he didn't remember the sleep. It was dreamless.

*

40

The sun's rays were crawling across the rangeland like a giant, fiery spider. They reached him and he winced, part of him actually thought it was a spider.

He heard crying.

Was he crying? He didn't think so. He listened.

The crying stopped.

A gust of wind whipped up the ashes of the house and blew them in a weird shape right before his eyes. A tall man in a black coat with no face.

The crying started again.

He sat up and cocked his ear. The dog imitated him.

Had the dog heard the crying?

He stood, as did the dog. The crying continued.

The dog waddled off on his little legs towards the ruin of the house. It stopped and looked back at Henry John. Then turned away and waddled further before stopping once more to look back.

Henry John followed. The tightness in his chest returned.

The crying stopped once again. But the dog was pawing the ground. Digging. Digging in the centre of the old house.

Henry John licked his lips and shivered. He shivered with that early morning coldness that always greets the sleeper. He realized he was thirsty. The dog! He should have watered the dog!

Forgetting for a moment that the dog was

41

digging, he grabbed a tin plate and one of the can-teens. He placed the tin plate on the floor and poured water into it.

Sunlight reflected off the water like a torch and he even turned to see if there was a beam of light shooting into the air.

The dog smelled the water and ran across, its legs working like crazy sending plumes of sand in every direction. The dog lapped up the water, tail wagging. When he'd finished he stood by the plate and raised his head to gaze at Henry John. A whole sentence of words passed between them in that gaze as the dog asked for more.

Henry John poured more water in the plate, sealed the canteen bottle and dropped it on the ground.

Then he walked across to where the dog had started digging. The ground was charcoal black. He saw blackened plates and mugs and a coffee pot. The log burner that had stood in the front of the stone fire-place glared at him with one large, black eye.

Under the ash his foot hit something smooth. Wood. It hadn't burned. A trap-door. The crying started again.

Brushing the ash and dust and soot out of the way, Henry John found the latch and lifted the door.

It was even blacker down there, the light unable

42

to penetrate the dust-laden air in the root cellar.

The crying intensified.

Henry John descended the steps into the cellar and was engulfed in the blackness.

The crying was ringing in his ears, it reverberated off the walls and reverberated off his head. Then he saw the baby, or rather, one flaying arm.

The child had been placed in a crib and wedged under a wooden pillar. The top had been covered over, obviously the dead woman had hoped that her child would escape the horror and would possibly be rescued at a later time – or die of starvation.

The father? The thought had not struck him before. Where was the body of the father? Had he been here?

Bending, he removed the cover and pulled the crib out. The baby's face was dirty with soot but unharmed. He carried it out into the bright sunlight and the baby stopped crying, too intent on shielding its eyes from the brilliance.

What the hell was he supposed to do now?

The dog sat at his feet and the baby crib rested in his powerful arms. He stared around, a bemused expression on his face.

There had to be other homesteads nearby, he thought. Yeah. There had to be. All I gotta do is find one.

Placing the crib on the ground, Henry John

opened one of the saddle-bag flaps and put the dog in it. Then, carefully lifting the crib, he mounted the horse and balanced the crib precariously across the pommel of his saddle. Holding it with one hand, and the reins with the other, he set off to look for a woman who could feed and, judging by the smell, maybe clean the baby up. William Henry John was not a baby man in truth. He felt uncomfortable having the infant with him. It wouldn't stop crying. He knew there was no point in trying to feed it with beans or water it with coffee.

He stopped and opened the canteen. Pouring some water into the small cap, he tried to get the baby to drink. All it would do was suck. So he poured the small droplets of water into the baby's mouth. The baby started coughing as it choked on the unexpected liquid.

Jumping off the saddle, Henry John took the baby out of the crib and placed it on his shoulder, gently tapping its back.

That's when he heard the gun cock behind him.

'Hold it right there, mister.'

Henry John stood exactly where he was. He heard the man dismount and walk up behind him.

'I got a baby here, mister,' Henry John said.

'Turn, real slow.'

Henry John turned. As soon as the man saw the baby he went white.

'What the hell d' you think you're doin?' he said.

'I found this little mite in the root cellar of a burned-out house, five six miles back. I'm a lookin' for a place to look after him.'

'That's my son!'

Henry John was speechless. He mutely handed over the small bundle.

'What about my wife and, and my other son?'

Henry John looked at the ground. He didn't have to say anything.

The man fell to his knees, clutching his precious child.

'I'm truly sorry, mister. I buried 'em both an' said a few words. There was nothing more I could do. It was the dog that showed me where the baby was.'

'You have Sally's dog?' the man asked.

'Sure do, in my saddle-bag.'

Henry John went to fetch the dog.

'Were you involved in their killin'?' the man asked.

'No, sir. I was not. If'n I were, I'd've killed the boy there, too.'

The man was trying to pull himself together.

'Was it Injuns?'

'I doubt it.' Henry John was about to mention rape, but decided against it. 'There were no arrows, an' as far as I know, Injuns don't wear boots.'

'I gotta go back there,' the man said.

'I don't think that's a good idea,' Henry John said. 'There's nothin' you can do fer them, you got your boy to look after, an' unless I'm mistaken, he's a mite hungry.'

The man thought about it for a couple of minutes.

Henry John added: 'We can always go back later.'

'You're right, mister, I wanna thank you fer, well, you know.'

Henry John nodded.

'There's a house over the next hill. The Smiths own it. We'll take Sean there.'

'Sean?'

'Yeah, that's my son. My name's Pete, Pete Hollander.'

The two men shook hands. 'Name's John, William Henry John.'

'Mighty pleased to meet, William.'

'Folks call me Henry John.'

'Henry John.'

Remounting their horses, Henry John followed Pete along the trail. The two men rode in silence. Pretty soon the house came into view. It was how he'd imaged Hollander's house would have looked before—

The tightness in his chest returned with a vengeance. Leaning forward in the saddle, his chin dropped on his chest and he panted, the rasping

46

sound cutting through the air like a knife.

Pete Hollander heard nothing of this as he was too busy trying to soothe his crying son.

Long before they reached the house, a man came into view holding a rifle. It was levelled and Henry John knew it was loaded.

Pete called out to the man, 'Ben! It's me, Pete.' The rifle was lowered and the two men rode on up to the house.

It took Henry John less than ten minutes to describe to both men and Ben's wife, Rose, what he'd discovered.

They were numb. Rose, because she'd lost her best friend, Ben because of the thought it could've been them.

'I'm goin' after them,' Pete said.

'I'll come with you,' Ben answered.

'No, you won't,' Henry John put in. 'You got a wife an' kid o' your own here, now you got another kid and a mutt. You ain't goin' nowheres. I'll go with Pete.'

'This ain't your fight, mister,' Pete said.

'I'm makin' it mine,' was all Henry John said. Rose took baby Sean to the back of the house and pretty soon he quit his bellyaching as she fed him fresh cow's milk.

'We'd best be leavin',' Henry John said. 'They've already got at least a day an' a half on us.'

47

'You're right, Henry John,' Pete said. 'I'll jus' say g'bye to my son.'

The two men, slightly refreshed and with plenty of water and food supplied by Ben and Rose King, set off to return to the Hollander place. Pete turned once, waved, and then never looked back again.

Henry John didn't even turn.

Four hours later, they reached the site of the killings. Pete dismounted and knelt by the side of his wife and son's graves. He bowed his head and, even from where Henry John stood at what he thought to be a respectful distance, he heard the racking sobs.

Henry John watched for a full minute, then he concentrated on the ground about him.

He walked a full circle around the charred remains of the house and barn until he came across the tracks he was hoping to find. They headed off into the mountains. He tried to count the horses, got to five and couldn't work out any more. But he could tell the direction.

Pete stood and walked back to his horse. Wiping the tears, he mounted and followed Henry John.

The two men exchanged life stories along the trail until sundown, then set about camp, lighting the fire and cooking. Pete was a dab hand at the bacon and eggs, the smell making their mouths water. They had enough eggs for another meal in the morning, then it was on to beans, bacon or the pot of stew Rose had included.

The two settled down to sleep. Pete didn't sleep a wink; it seemed as soon as he dropped off he woke again.

Henry John closed his eyes. His breathing was coming in laboured gulps, panting, he again tried to suck in the cooling air, but it was never enough. He slept.

Next morning, Pete had already stoked up the fire before Henry John woke up. It was still dark, but to the east the sky was a deep red, heralding dawn. Birds sang and flew around looking for food to feed their young before the heat of the day arrived.

Eggs and bacon was served up, fresh coffee poured. To Henry John, the coffee was nectar. He'd forgotten how good fresh coffee tasted.

They saddled up and in the early-morning watery light they followed the tracks. Within an hour, they found a camp-site. The fire was still smouldering, they hadn't even bothered to put it out.

Pete dismounted and walked around, looking for signs as to how many men were involved. As far as he was concerned, it could have been a hundred and he'd still chase them down.

To inexperienced trackers, as the two men were, it was impossible to tell how many men there were.

Henry John thought six, Pete thought more. They rode on.

The tracks they followed showed that, in fact, there were six riders. And they weren't in any hurry.

Henry John and Pete spurred their mounts on. With luck, they both secretly thought, they might even sight the riders soon. Hopefully, by the time they reached the mountains.

It was Pete who saw the dust cloud ahead first. He reined in his animal and pointed it out to Henry John. A smile crept on their faces, not the usual kind of smile, not one tinged with happiness or pleasure. It was a resigned, fatalistic smile of the end of the road.

Breathing became difficult again. The pain in Henry John's chest was intense. He couldn't understand why it came on in these fits and starts.

The heat of the noonday sun beat down on them relentlessly. It attacked them from below as well, as the desert sand heated up and boiled the very air they tried to breathe.

They had no plan.

Reining in his animal, Henry John told Pete they'd better think of something, and fast. The ideal situation was to get ahead of the riders, which meant heading off west and circling around – which could take the rest of the day.

There seemed to be no alternative. They set their

sights on the distant mountains, hoping to find a good place to bushwhack the men ahead.

Without stopping for either rest or food, the two men made a detour, keeping their eyes triangulated from their position to the men ahead and the mountains.

Night fell.

The quiet of the desert was only broken by the hoofs of their horses crunching gently into the sand. This was soon replaced by the distant calls of coyotes and wolves baying to the moon before starting their nocturnal forage of life and death.

The mountains loomed closer. The moonlight reflected off the rock, throwing strange and eerie shadows which set the hairs on the back of Henry John's neck bristling.

Reaching the mountains, they were sure they were ahead of the riders. Tethering their animals, Pete and Henry John clambered up the rock face to get a better view of the surrounding country, and to see if they could spot the group.

Sure enough, they were ahead of their quarry. Less than half a mile away they caught the faint glow of a camp fire. They could even see the sparks lifted into the air, a bright red, glow in the black sky.

'They're camped out for the night,' Pete said.

'Yeah. We better decide on how we're gonna play this.' Henry John sat and pondered. Neither man was a killer – to the best of their knowledge.

'Either we ambush 'em as they ride through the pass, or we attack when they're asleep,' Pete said.

'I reckon we do it in the dark,' Henry John said. 'They ain't likely to post no guards, now are they?'

'Suits me,' Pete replied.

'We'll wait a few more hours, make sure they're asleep.'

'S'posing they ain't the ones?' Pete said.

'They are. Don't ask me how I know that. I jus' know they are.'

'Reckon we should get some shut eye.' Pete took a coin from his pocket.

'Heads, I sleep first, tails, you do. OK?'

'Sure.'

Pete flicked the coin in the air. Henry John watched as it spun lazily, reflecting the moon's glow as it reached the top of the throw, then just as lazily spun back to earth.

'Tails.'

'Wake me in an hour,' Henry John said. He settled himself against a rock and tilted his Stetson over his eyes, folded his arms and fell asleep within minutes.

Images of his dead family etched themselves on the inside of his eyelids. His eyes were moving rapidly from side to side like an eraser trying to rub the pictures out. To no avail. The faster his eyes went, the clearer the pictures became. Then the sound arrived.

He could hear his first wife talking to him, cooing in his ear, putting his meal on the kitchen table, throwing her arms around his waist, snuggling up to him in bed.

Then his second wife appeared, but not before he saw his first wife dead again, in glorious colour, in minute detail. He heard her last breath.

Then he heard the thunder of the cattle. Saw their flared nostrils, heard the wood splinter and watched as his second family died. He was willing himself to wake up, to get rid of this nightmare, his own voice was saying wake up, wake up, wake up.

'Wake up, Henry John. Wake up.'

The rough hands shook his shoulders and he stared into the face of Pete. It couldn't have been an hour, but, checking his pocket watch, he saw that it had been two.

Henry John sat up. The cold night air freezing the sweat that ran down his face. The dampness of his clothes turned to ice.

'Seems you were dreamin',' Pete said.

'Dreamin' ain't what I'd call it.'

'I think the riders have settled down. Can't make out any movement.'

Henry John stood and gazed into the distance. 'Hard to tell from here,' he said.

'I bin closer, much closer. They'd bin drinkin', I could smell it and hear their snorin',' Pete said. 'Let's get this over with then.'

The two men checked their weapons, rifles ready, guns loaded. Henry John took out a long, hunting knife and looked at it in the moonlight. The cruel, steel blade winked back at him, telling him it was ready.

Carefully, they made their way down the rock face onto the flatlands once more.

Henry John could hear the sound of millions of grains of sand grinding together as he walked. He heard the leather of his holster squeak as it rubbed on his belt. Then he heard his breathing. Shallow, slow and painful. He looked towards Pete, but the man heard nothing. The old panic crept into Henry John's head and wouldn't leave. The panic that said if you don't get more air in your lungs, you're gonna die!

He opened his mouth wide, taking deep breaths, then remembered his mother, closed his mouth and breathed deeply through his nose. It still wasn't enough. His chest hardly moved.

Then it was gone.

Slowly they moved forward, their boots crunching into the sand and hitting rock. To Henry John it sounded like thunder, the noise reverberating through his skull. Pete heard nothing. His gaze was fixed on the camp fire ahead. He had only one thought in his mind. Death.

They were within twenty feet of the camp site now. Henry John moved to the left as Pete, wordlessly, moved to the right.

Henry John took out his hunting knife. It winked back at him again, unbelievably, he winked at it.

Crouching, the two men moved in at an angle. The sleeping men, snoring loudly, were in a circle round the fire, their horses were tethered out of the radius of the fire's light.

Henry John swallowed. It seemed to calm his nerves. He began to have doubts these men were the ones who'd killed Pete's wife and son. He pushed them to the back of his mind. He was sure. There could be no doubt.

Kneeling, he slit the throat of the nearest man. There was no sound. The blood pumped out on to the ground, it looked black. Some of it hissed into the fire.

The dying man's eyes opened – briefly – then closed again. Henry John moved on to the next body and did the same.

The silence was broken by the sharp crack of gunfire. Pete Hollander didn't have a knife.

Three down, Henry John thought. Two more to go.

Before he could reach his third victim, the

remaining two men were wide awake and on their feet, guns drawn.

Henry John dropped his knife and went for his gun. Too late.

He saw Pete go down as one of the men fired. The other man turned towards Henry John and levelled his pistol.

Everything slowed down from that point in.

He felt the butt of his Colt in the palm of his hand, felt his elbow bend as the gun slowly came out of the leather holster. His thumb cocked back the hammer at the same instant and his right index finger caressed the trigger. He brought the gun to bear at hip level, not waiting to extend his arm, which was moving too slowly.

Henry John watched as the bullet left the muzzle of his pistol and flew through the air before exploding into the chest of the man opposite him.

He brought his left hand up and cocked the hammer for the second time. Swivelling the gun to his left, he loosed a second shot. The bullet moved even slower this time. Henry John could see the ragged filings on the end of the bullet as it flew towards its target.

The man stood, feet apart, pistol levelled, pointing straight at Henry John's heart. Before he could pull the trigger, Henry John's bullet caught him in the stomach. The man doubled up on impact and flopped back downwards, sitting on the camp fire.

Within seconds, he was a blazing inferno as his trousers, shirt and vest caught fire. Henry John had time to think about how he'd caught fire so quickly. The man's clothes were covered in grease and dirt.

Henry John watched as the man, forgetting the slug in his gut, ran off into the darkness before falling to the ground, writhing in agony trying to smother the flames.

His screams pierced the night air and remained with Henry John for a long time.

Then it was quiet.

Panting, hardly able to breathe, Henry John walked across to the prone form of Pete.

He was dead. The single shot had caught him in the head. He never knew anything about it.

Once again, Henry John was on his own.

He searched through the men's saddle-bags and found jewellery, watches and wallets. One of the wallets bore the gold-leafed inscription:

TO MY DARLING PETE
FROM YOUR EVER LOVING WIFE

Henry John picked up his knife, cleaned it on the sand and slipped it back into the buckskin sheath on the rear of his gun-belt.

He released the horses and let them run, then he went for his spade.

He'd bury Pete, repeating the same thoughts he'd had when he'd buried his wife and son.

CHAPTER TWO

Lying on his back, near the camp fire, Henry John felt fingers on his chest.

He'd spent a restless night. After burying Pete – he'd left the other men for the buzzards – he'd made his way back to their camp site. In a daze, he'd lit the fire and boiled some coffee. He could neither feel the heat of the fire nor taste the coffee.

His eyelids felt as if they weighed a ton. He had to sleep. But he didn't want to sleep. He felt that if he did, he might never wake up again.

The dreams returned, beckoning him. Dreams into nightmares were but a flick of the eye.

He saw, rather than felt, himself flying. He couldn't see what he was flying over, but he knew he was flying. The pain in his chest returned with a vengeance, gasping for breath, his nostrils flaring, he opened his eyes and saw himself lying there.

Henry John woke up with a start. So clear, so intense had been the nightmare that both hands felt for the ground.

Again, he was bathed in sweat, rivulets of icy water running down the back of his neck.

He sat up. It took him a few minutes to remember where he was and what he'd done. For the first time in weeks, he rummaged through his saddle-bags and found the tobacco pouch. Rolling a thin cigarette, he pulled out a burning stick and lit up.

The acrid smoke burnt its way down the back of his throat and steered a course through his lungs. He drew deeply again, his head swam as the nicotine found its way into his bloodstream. Henry John thought he was going to fall over. He didn't. The dizziness lasted only a few seconds.

He had no trouble inhaling deeply on the cigarette; maybe he should smoke more often, he thought. Then smiled.

Dawn again. The sun stuck its head up over the horizon and tentatively dipped its long fingers into the oncoming day to see what it was like. As ever, it approved, and the head of the sun rose majestically into the air.

Birds were already singing. Henry John tried to see one, but he couldn't. All he could do was hear them.

He ate. While eating, he decided he'd better

return Pete's horse and pass on yet more bad news to the couple who had his baby son. What was the kid's name? Sean. Yeah, that was it. Sean.

He flicked the stub of the cigarette into the fire and then kicked sand over the flames.

He poured a generous amount of water into his Stetson and walked across to his horse. The animal's ears flicked up at his approach, and it gently snorted and pawed the ground before burying its head in the hat, lapping up the water. Then he watered Pete's horse.

Saddling up, Henry John tied the reins of the second horse to his saddle and set off.

The air was clear and crisp and the heat from the sun gently bathed his face and the back of his hands. A tolerable warmth he knew would grow in intensity as the day wore on.

The long, winding trail spread out before him. He was in no hurry to deliver misery. He felt the breath of a breeze lick his face, saw the grains of sand roll against each other forming new ripples here, losing old ones there. The breeze grew stronger, filled the air with sand and the clear, blue sky took on a greenish tinge as the yellow sand rose in small billowy clouds.

It was no longer a breeze. It was a wind.

He halted the horses and reached into his saddle-bags for a bandanna. Tying it round his nose and mouth, the crimson bandanna billowed in the wind. The sand got into his ears, his eyes, up his nose and in his mouth. He ground his teeth together and listened to the crunch and grate as the sand lodged between them.

He stopped again. The wind – which had sprung up from the breeze which had sprung up from nothing – was now a howling gale. The sand no longer gently billowed. It cut through the air like a million sharp knives slashing at the exposed skin of his hands and around his eyes.

It was pointless going on. He couldn't even open his eyes, let alone see anything.

Henry John dismounted and, forcing his Winchester into the sand, he tied the two horses to it. He found blankets and covered the horses' heads in an attempt to shield them. They shied away, but realized what he was doing and stood placidly, turning their backs towards the direction of the strongest winds.

Using the sailcloth that doubled as tent and groundsheet, Henry John covered himself over and sat in the middle of the desert, in the middle of a sand storm – to wait it out.

He soon fell into a deep, trance-like sleep. The howl and whistle of the wind accompanied by the rat-a-tat-tat of the sand hitting the sailcloth like a Gatling gun, went unheard.

He panted. Opened his mouth wide. Closed it. Breathed deeply through his nose as he dreamed.

For some strange reason, the face tattooed on his eyelids was that of baby Sean. He was flanked on either side by Ben and Rose King. They were seated on the veranda of their little house, just staring. The picture vanished to be replaced by Sean in his crib in the root cellar. This dissolved into Pete's dead face staring up at him, saying, 'kill the boy too, why don't you.'

Henry John answered the voice by saying he hadn't killed his mother, he'd only killed the outlaws.

The voice and the face left him. He was looking into a whiskey tumbler, leaning against a bar top in an unknown saloon in an unknown town.

His coat felt so very heavy, he could hardly keep it on, he could hardly stand. He'd have to sit and take the weight off his shoulders. The blue serge overcoat that fell from shoulder to ankle in length, weighed more than he could bear.

The band around his chest returned and he gasped out loud in pain. He couldn't suck the air in long enough. It kept wheezing out before it could do him any good.

The weight was intolerable and the sound of the shot woke him up.

It was dark. Stifling and dark. He couldn't move.

The weight on his shoulders wasn't the overcoat at all, it was the sailcloth. He hadn't realized it was so heavy. He could hardly move it.

Opening a slit in the front, he saw only yellow. The yellow ran in and he watched it as, like an hour-glass, it began to fill up the inside of the sailcloth.

Henry John remembered where he was and why he was there. Panic filled him. Then he relaxed. The thought of being buried alive no longer worried him. He felt calm. If this was how it was going to be, then let it be.

On the other hand, he thought, I'd better see if I can get out first. No point dying yet if there ain't no need.

He forced his right hand through the slowly-filling slit in the sailcloth and pushed upwards.

His hand reached the open air. He brought his left hand up and sat there moving his arms in small semi-circles, moving the sand away from his shoulders.

He was free. Stepping back into the blazing sun-light, he looked around him. He couldn't see the rifle, but the horses were still there. He dug down to where the reins met the cool of the rifle barrel and pulled the weapon out.

Where he'd sat, a huge dome had built up that rose slightly more than five feet. To his left, it towered to a height of over twelve feet. He'd been lucky.

The smooth terrain he had ridden into was now covered with dunes of varying height. It was disorientating, and he would have lost all sense of direction, had it not been for the sun and the mountains.

Resuming his journey and with a heavy heart, Henry John walked the horses on. The going was difficult, the sand was deep and loose; before it had been hard-packed and easier to navigate.

His path meandered, looking for the firmest ground and the shortest route.

It took him five more long hours to reach the grassy plain and sight the Kings' homestead. They were out on the veranda watching him ride in alone. He pulled up outside the picket fence and dismounted. They both looked at him and when they saw his face, they didn't need to ask any questions.

'Come in, Henry John. You look tired,' Rose said to him. 'Ben'll take care of the horses.'

Wearily, Henry John followed Rose. Before he entered he removed his jacket and shook half the desert out of it. Then he removed his boots and shook the other half out.

'See you been married before,' she observed.

'Only the twice, ma'am,' Henry John replied, and removed his hat.

Coffee was boiling and some cookies were hurriedly placed in front of him.

Rose sat and watched him eat and drink. She was

dying to ask questions, but she refrained. There was something about the man – an aura, she thought – that prevented her.

Ben walked in. 'Horses are fed and watered. I put your saddle by the stable, but I brought your saddle-bags in.'

'Thanks,' Henry John said. He reached into the saddle-bags and brought out several sacks which he placed on the side table. He emptied the contents of one and Rose took a sharp intake of breath.

'My, my,' she said. 'Aren't they the most beautiful jewels you ever did see?'

She leant forward. Henry John could see she was dying to pick them up and feel them.

'Go ahead, ma'am,' he said. 'Take 'em, they're yours.'

She stared at his face long and hard, not sure if he was fooling around or serious.

'Go ahead. Take 'em. I took 'em off the outlaws who killed Pete.'

Rose put her hands to her face. She already knew Pete was dead, but to be told – that was certainty.

'I buried him, ma'am, an' said the same words as I said for his wife and son. What about Sean?'

Rose looked to her husband. He nodded.

'He'll be safe with us, we'll bring him up as our own. When he's old enough, I'll tell him,' she said softly.

'Reckon these here trinkets'll go a long way for helping out with his room an' board,' Henry John said.

'You're welcome to stay on a whiles,' Ben King said.

'Thank you kindly, but I'd best be off. I seen too much sorrow of late. I'll settle down again one day, but not now.'

'I respect your decision, Henry John. There'll always be a place here for you, if you're ever in the vicinity.'

'I appreciate that, Ben.'

'You can't go just yet,' Rose said. 'You'll need a change of clothing at the very least.'

Henry John looked down at his clothes. He'd not noticed the blood before. He was covered in it.

'Reckon you're right there, ma'am,' he said.

'You get those things off and I'll wash them. Ben's about your size. I'll dig some of his things out 'til yours are ready.'

Rose was never happier than when she was busy fussing over something, and getting Henry John looking respectable again was just what she needed to be doing. She left the two men alone.

Henry John undressed down to his underwear while Ben got him fresh trousers and a shirt. Rose re-entered and took the filthy garments outside to the washtub.

'Whiskey?' Ben asked.

'Thanks.'

Ben poured two generous glasses and the two men sat and chewed fat.

Within twenty minutes, Henry John was asleep again, his mouth open wide, gulping in vast quantities of oxygen that didn't quite seem to be enough, never quite made it into his chest.

Ben and Rose didn't notice anything.

Henry John spent the entire night on the only armchair in the house. Ben and Rose left him where he was. He didn't hear the crying of young Sean who waited impatiently to be fed, nor did he hear the rain thundering down on the tin roof, fit to wake the dead.

Henry John dreamed again. It followed the same format as before, coloured images flashed across his brain, some stopped for brief moments before flitting off again; the only constant was breathing.

The background to all the images was his laboured breathing that had now added a slight, hollow sounding whistle.

There was something there he couldn't quite comprehend. Something just out of reach, but it was getting closer. He knew that.

Rose cooked a breakfast the likes of which Henry John hadn't enjoyed for longer than he could remember. Ben joined them. He'd been working in the barn, Rose had collected the eggs herself while Henry John slept. Young Sean was asleep in the crib. To all intents and purposes, there permeated an atmosphere of contentment, of normality.

The nightmares in Henry John's head began to appear in the daylight.

He'd thought he was imagining it at first, that he hadn't woken up yet, that he'd only dreamed he had. Yet, between Ben and Rose sat a man he'd never seen before.

His jacket was off and his hands were covered in blood. He held a sharp knife in his left hand, the kind that medical people sometimes used. The man looked sad, he was talking to someone, not to Henry John, but about him.

He couldn't hear the words. The man's lips moved almost imperceptively beneath his neatly-trimmed moustache. He kept looking to one side and then down again. Henry John tried to catch the man's eyes, but he melted away. Only Ben and Rose sat opposite him.

'I said, are you all right, Henry John?' Rose was looking at him with a puzzled expression on her face.

'Yeah. Yeah, sorry, I was miles away, I could've sworn—' he stopped short.

'Could've sworn what, Henry John?' Ben asked.

'Nothin'. This sure is a damn fine breakfast, ma'am. I can't remember the last time—'

Henry John stopped once more. He did remember the last time he'd eaten a breakfast like this. His first wife had cooked it two days before she'd been killed. She was now sitting in between Rose and Ben.

Henry John jumped up. 'I gotta be goin' now,' he said.

'There's no hurry, surely,' Rose said.

'I wanna thank you for your hospitality, but I gotta get to the coast. I gotta see that ocean, then everything'll be all right.'

'I'll saddle up for you, Henry John, while you get ready,' Ben said as they finished eating.

Henry John buckled his gun-belt on, checked the pistol was on safety, grabbed his battered hat and jacket and walked toward the front door.

Rose stepped in his path. 'You take care, Henry John. And you come visit us when you've seen that ocean.'

'Thank you, ma'am, I sure will. An' you look after that young nipper.'

'I will.' Rose leaned forward and placed her lips on Henry John's cheek. He blushed, then coughed with embarrassment.

Ben rode up on Henry John's horse to save further talk.

The two men shook hands and Henry John galloped off into the Plains as if his life depended on it.

Ben and Rose King stood and watched him go. They waited for him to turn back and wave.

He didn't.

Henry John rode as if the very devil himself was on his tail. There was more going on in his head than he could fathom. And he was scared.

Very scared.

Thinking more of his horse than himself, he reined the animal to a walking pace and settled himself in the saddle.

The Plains rolled on for miles in every direction, a flat expanse of green, swaying grassland, punctuated by trees and the odd boulder. Cactus, rising high into the air, with silhouettes like a man with arms raised, framed the horizon.

It was time, he thought, to re-evaluate his life. There had been too much sorrow of late. It seemed that everywhere he went, tragedy dogged his footsteps.

Out here on the Plains, a man felt his true value. The insignificance was all too apparent. Surely there was no way man could pollute the Plains with his evil ways? Nature was too powerful, too all-consuming and just to allow that to happen.

Noon time again, the sun blazed. There were white wispy clouds scudding along on a wind that didn't reach ground level. Henry John halted his horse and dismounted. Using his sailcloth, he rigged a shelter and gathered kindling and dry wood for the fire.

Striking his flint, the kindling ignited within seconds, and adding the wood piece by piece, he soon had a fire going.

Taking out the soot-blackened enamelled coffee pot, he half-filled it with water, added the beans and suspended it over the fire.

It was time for a smoke.

He rolled a cigarette and lit it before lying back under the shelter. It wasn't cooler under the sail-cloth, but it kept the direct sunlight from him.

It was quiet. Eerily quiet. Silent as the tomb. He remembered his father. Strange, he thought, how one expression can conjure up so many thoughts and reminiscences.

His father always told him that children should be seen and not heard, and to keep as silent as a tomb unless spoken to.

Henry John had no idea at that time what a tomb was or how silent it was. He remembered the beating he got with his father's leather strap when he dared to ask the question.

He felt the pain again, not on his naked buttocks, but his chest. He looked down at his body spread out before him. The pain in his chest was like a lead weight pressing down. It was difficult to fill his lungs, the effort of both breathing in and trying to expand his chest was just too much.

Exhausted with the effort, he fell asleep.

Dreamtime.

He watched the rodeo clowns as they jinxed and danced and swerved to attract the attention of the giant, black Brahma. The crowd was cock-a-hoop, the rider had stayed on the beast's back for the required minute and then ejected himself into the air as far away from those killer hoofs as he could get – which was not quite far enough. But that's what the crowd liked.

The bull, snorting steam from his nostrils, was not intent on trampling the rider to death. It never even entered his brain. The binding straps that were around his huge neck was what he was now trying to get rid of.

Head down, eyes ablaze, the bull thrust his rear legs outwards and upwards with a kick that sent a swish through the air. Dust rose and fell as the creature danced its futile way around the arena. Women screamed and laughed, men drank beer, bronco-busters got themselves ready for their dice with death.

The brass band struck up Dixie in a tempo that was just a tad too quick, but nobody was bothered. The sun shone, the beer and the food was aplenty and people were happy.

The junior event was next on the agenda and William Henry John was the last rider in it. The boy sweated, not from the heat, not from the thrill, but from sheer terror.

The six-month-old calves the boys would ride seemed, to him, every bit as ferocious as the Brahma.

It was not his idea to ride.

He was riding for his father. He was riding because his father couldn't. The broken leg suffered during his youth had not been set properly, leaving him with a stiff leg that had little feeling in it.

Henry John rode through his father.

He sat abreast the brown and white calf, rope wrapped tightly around his right wrist. He was doing his best not to piss in his pants. Surrounded by six or seven rodeo workers, they opened the wooden catch-gate and thumped the calf on the rump to get him going.

The animal shot out of the holding pen as if Satan was on his tail. Henry John's head was thrown back with a jerk, followed by the rest of his body – he didn't even make a second.

He landed with a thud on the ground, all the wind knocked out of him. He couldn't get his breath. The air had been driven out of him so severely that he couldn't breathe. He remembered the smells, meat being barbequed, candy, coffee, and not being able to breathe. The smell of the coffee was strongest, hanging in the air like a brown cloud.

He couldn't breathe. Couldn't breathe – the smell of the coffee.

He woke up with a start. The white sailcloth was a shroud. He was dead, he felt certain.

He sat up, knocking the makeshift tent-pole over. He was covered in the sailcloth, fighting to get his breath.

Arms going like a windmill, he managed to get himself free. The air came into his lungs like a tidal wave. He was bathed in sweat. He'd been dreaming, he realized. The smell of the coffee was the coffee pot on the fire that had boiled dry, giving off a sharp, bitter aroma.

He mopped his brow. His shirt was soaked so he took it off, spreading it over the tall grass to dry off in the sun. He rebuilt his shelter and, taking the canteen with him, he crawled back inside. All thoughts of drinking coffee had vanished.

He rested for another hour, half awake, half asleep, but dreamless, for which he was grateful.

His shirt had dried; it felt stiff, but dry. He put it back on and looked to the sky. Still clear, the wispy clouds scudded along.

He saw the birds to the west, flying in ever diminishing circles, getting lower and lower until they were lost from view.

Vultures.

Vultures didn't fly much unless food was in the offing. He'd seen trees full of the ugly things in his time, just sitting, watching, waiting.

Whatever was over to the west, it was dead. Of that he was sure.

He saddled up and rode on, heading for where he'd last seen the birds. It took an hour to reach the large, flattened trail. What he saw took his breath away – literally – and made him feel both sick and ashamed.

The stench alone was horrific enough without the sight of the steam rising lazily into the air.

It was a massacre. A senseless, bloody, one-sided massacre.

For as far as the eye could see were the rotting, stinking corpses of buffalo.

They'd been skinned, but their heads were all too visible. Young, old, bulls, cows, all dead for their pelts.

Henry John realized then that man could pollute the Plains, and already had.

He reached for his spade, then stopped himself. There was no way he could even begin to bury this herd. There must be over five-hundred dead animals. Enough meat going to waste to feed an average tribe of Plains Indians for ten years. Gone. Wiped out.

He felt the sting of tears. The tight band around his chest made the sobbing difficult. Even out here, he thought, in the middle of nowhere, in God's green land, the evil fingers of man stretched and annihilated everything they came into contact with.

Pretty soon, man's best friend would be the vulture.

William Henry John rode on, his heart heavy, but also filled with a new resolve.

Red Rock was a fairly large town, nestled on the western side of the Sierra Nevadas. It was inexplicably a thriving community.

Surrounded by rich, fertile farmlands, as well as prairie for the cattle, it was within easy reach of the coast, being only two days' ride away.

The throb of the town could be felt even before Henry John reached it. Smoke from the myriad chimneys billowed into the air, the woody aroma making his mouth water.

He'd never seen a town as big or so bustling as this in his life. Sure, he'd seen the etchings in magazines from back East. Large brick buildings, paved streets, even street lights. But to experience it was another thing.

Not all the buildings in Red Rock were brick built. Some, the older, probably the founding part of the town, still resembled the towns of the old west. But farther away from the centre, the more modern, two- and sometimes three-storey brick buildings rose majestically into the air.

The main street in town was paved, the streets leading off were the usual hard-packed dirt with wooden boardwalks. It was one of these streets that Henry John rode down, looking for a cheap hotel.

The Yellow Rose was just such a hotel.

He checked in and went to his room. It was perfectly square with a large window facing the distant mountains. Outside the window was a balcony. Henry John opened the double windows and stepped onto it. The hustle and bustle of the town went on in the street below. There was what appeared to be a cattle stockade at one end of what he now realized was a dead-end street. A cattle auction was in full swing; he could just make out the fast-talking of the auctioneer as he banged his gavel on a hand-held piece of wood as each deal was struck.

He went back into the room. A large, brass-headed double bed filled most of the room. A small table and chair and a wardrobe with a chest of drawers attached to it, completed the furniture. The pitcher and basin, with a small hand towel and bar of soap, sat atop the chest.

Splashing his face with the surprisingly cool water, Henry John thought about getting himself fixed up with a job.

There must be a million opportunities in this town, he thought, for someone willing to do an honest day's work for an honest day's pay.

He left the room, refreshed and looked for a cafe. He was spoilt for choice. There seemed to be a cafe or a saloon on every street corner.

There were general stores, hardware stores, clothes stores, a milliner with some of the fanciest hats Henry John had ever seen, bristling with feathers or fruit or stuffed birds. Banks galore; it seemed every association had its own bank.

He found a saloon that looked quiet enough and ordered a beer. Sitting at one of the large, round tables, he started to wonder what sort of life it'd be to just stay in this town, forget about the wide, open spaces.

The beer was good, cold and he could taste the malt. It'd been a long time since he'd enjoyed a beer so much.

Limiting himself to one, he left and walked around town. Breathing in the atmosphere, it was like being in heaven.

The call of the ocean was too great. He'd no idea what to expect, or indeed, why he wanted to see it.

He just knew he had to get there – and soon.

Walking back to the hotel, he took his horse over to a trough and let the animal drink. He'd been careful to let him rest before filling his belly with water. He looked at the horse. Old now, but faithful. Perhaps he should put him out to grass for a few weeks, give him a rest.

Later, maybe. Right now, he wanted to see the ocean. He needed to see the ocean.

Henry John spent a restless night. The problem was the bed was far too soft. He felt as if he was being swallowed up whole.

In the early hours of the morning, after spending two or three hours tossing and turning, Henry John pulled a blanket off the bed and settled down to sleep on the floor.

The floorboards, although unforgiving and even harder than the nights he'd spent under the stars, was infinitely preferable to the soft mattress.

When sleep eventually came, the dreamtime returned. As before, the dreams started to flit from one thing to another at the speed of light. Images appeared and disappeared. Visions began and melted.

Gradually, his subconscious settled on a dream to concentrate on.

Henry John was seated at the foot of his mother's

bed. The blinds and the curtains were drawn. On the bedside table, an oil-lamp, wick turned down low, flickered, giving off a sickening yellow light.

The room was full of people. His father sat on the side of the bed holding his mother's hand. Near the door, and behind Henry John, two women stood with handkerchiefs pressed to their noses, quietly weeping.

The pastor was there, on the opposite side of the bed. He wore a purple scarf and was reading from the bible.

Henry John sat on a chair, his legs not reaching the floor. He was bored. He started swinging his legs to and fro, to and fro. His father looked at him and glared. That look, Henry John remembered for a long time.

Although he didn't realize it at the time, that look conveyed anger, hatred and disappointment.

The sheets were pulled up over his mother's face. He couldn't see her. There was a smell in the room he didn't like, a rank, sour smell that made Henry John hold his nose.

He said, 'Poo!' out loud.

One of the women behind him grabbed his small hand and yanked him out of the bedroom. He was told to stay in his room and not come out until he was told to.

He stayed there the rest of that day, all night, and

most of the next day. He wondered what it was he'd done wrong.

In the early evening, his father came into the room. He looked pale and there were red rings round his eyes. Henry John thought he looked like a sad rodeo clown and he almost laughed out loud.

His father informed him that his wife, Henry John's mother, was dead.

Henry John sat and looked at his father. Incomprehension was written all over the little boy's face.

'But who will look after me now?' he asked.

His father stood and without looking back, left the room.

Henry John fell into a deep sleep that night, hugging his doll, the doll his mother had made for him to sleep with. The same doll that had so angered his father.

He remembered gripping it so tight, the knuckles on his hands turned white with the effort. He remembered also, his lack of breath, the inability to breathe in and out like a normal person.

He called out in his sleep, but no one came. He cried and cried, but no one came.

Henry John woke up. He was gripping the leg of the bed so tightly his fingers and wrists hurt, his knuckles had turned white and he was crying.

From the room next to his, someone was banging

all hell on the connecting wall, telling him to keep the noise down or he'd blow his goddamned head off.

Gasping for air, Henry John let go of the bed leg and sat up. The now familiar beads of sweat that cascaded down his face were ignored in the effort of keeping alive.

Tomorrow, he said to himself, the ocean!

CHAPTER THREE

The sun crept over the balcony and lit up the room in a bright glare. Already traffic was moving on the street below.

Henry John opened his eyes and looked around the room. The ceiling, painted white, looked a long way off. His back was stiff, as was his shoulder. He sat up, easing his aching muscles, working his stiff shoulder.

Breakfast was a solitary affair. The small cafe was deserted. Downing his second cup of coffee, he paid the bill and went back to the hotel room. The stiffness in his joints was still there. He tried to ease them as he walked but the muscles wouldn't respond.

He paused at a hitching rail – had to – the pain in his chest was more ferocious than he could remember.

Breathing deeply through his nose – thanks mother – he calmed himself down. He didn't notice, but people gave him funny looks as they passed. Some of the women out getting the daily stores crossed the street rather than walk past him.

Breathing steadily again, he entered the hotel lobby, rang the bell on the counter and waited for the clerk. He paid for his night's lodging and went back to his room to pack up.

The horse had been well-groomed. His coat shone in the early morning sun. They were pleased to see each other. Sliding his saddle-bags over the back of the saddle, Henry John mounted. He sat tall for a while, feeling good, letting everyone see this was no ordinary cowboy on no ordinary horse.

Slowly, he set off. Past the Yellow Rose Hotel, past the banks and general stores until he was level with the sheriff's office-cum-town jail.

The window was plastered with Wanted posters. An idea lit up in his head. Bounty Hunting.

It had never occurred to him before. He wasn't a man who sought out violence or danger, but of late it had seemed to find him.

Tying his horse to a hitching post he walked over to the window. The rogue's gallery of hand-drawn likenesses seemed to fit most people. Some so ugly, you couldn't possibly miss them on a dark night with your eyes shut.

Henry John smiled to himself. People's imaginations sure went haywire when trying to describe someone who'd just robbed a bank, or rustled some of their cattle.

He entered the office. The sheriff, a small, squat man, was leaning back in his chair. A mug of coffee was steaming on his desk, but the sheriff was intent on polishing his handgun. The man didn't even look up as Henry John closed the door behind him.

'Mornin', stranger,' the sheriff said.

'Mornin', Sheriff.'

'What can I do for you?'

'Aim to collect me some bounty,' Henry John said.

The sheriff raised his eyes and took Henry John in.

'You caught somebody?'

'Nope.'

'Got somebody in mind?'

'Nope.'

'Then what do you want?'

'Figured you might let me have copies o' some o' them Wanted posters you got in the window. Maybe I can find one or two o' them.'

'You done this before, stranger?'

'Nope.'

The sheriff looked Henry John up and down once again.

'OK, I'll sort some out for you.' The sheriff stood and went across to a large, wooden drawer. With some effort, he pulled the drawer out. It was crammed with Wanted posters.

'Mind if 'n I help myself?' Henry John asked.

'Be my guest,' the sheriff replied, glad to get back to polishing his gun.

Henry John squatted in front of the drawer and began to look through the posters. There must be over a thousand, he thought to himself. The first thing he learned was not to bother with any poster with a reward of less than five-hundred dollars.

That whittled the amount down somewhat. Then he decided not to take any poster that involved more than one person – male or female.

This made his task even easier. Pretty soon he was holding a pile of thirty posters.

He closed the drawer and turned back to the sheriff.

'OK if I take these?'

'Sure is. Makes my job easier.'

Henry John tipped his hat and left the office.

Rolling the posters up, he stuffed them into his saddle-bags and rode out of Red Rock.

The trail he followed headed due west. He was in no hurry. The scenery was different to anything he'd experienced before and he spent time looking around.

When the sun was directly overhead, he decided to camp down and cook some chow and brew up. The sailcloth came in handy again as he sheltered from the noon-day sun. Getting himself comfortable, he went through the posters with a fine-tooth comb. One or two he threw out of the pile.

He stared at one particular poster for a long time. The man, known as Black Jake, was wanted in California and Nevada for armed robbery, rape and suspected arson.

The last robbery had been in Red Rock, where he'd wounded a hardware store owner and stolen guns and ammo and seventy-five dollars; that had been only two weeks ago.

Henry John decided to try and find this man.

He had very little to go on, only a gut feeling that he couldn't shake.

The face that stared back at him was covered with black beard, the eyes were penetrating, almost demonic, and a thrill of fear ran down Henry John's spine. The reward was one-thousand dollars. Quite a sum for one man, Henry John thought. Someone sure wanted him caught.

Time for a nap. He felt his eyelids begin to close and although he fought it for a while, he gave up and settled back under the sailcloth. The wave of sudden tiredness that swept over him was alarming.

It was happening more and more recently, and as he thought about that, the dull throb in his chest began again.

He fell asleep. The dreams came thick and fast like a kaleidoscope of colour and images, flashing too quickly for him to comprehend. Every now and then a face would halt in front of his eyes, just long enough to recognize, but not name.

The images flashed so fast he was beginning to feel dizzy in his own dream, then they stopped.

He was lying in a field of tall grass, totally naked except for his hat. The soft green grass was caressing his body. The woman beside him was asleep, her chest gently rising and falling. He couldn't see her face, only the milky softness of her breasts and stomach and long, long legs.

The grass began to tickle and he scratched. It tickled again and again he scratched. It felt as if something was crawling over him.

Henry John woke up with a start. Something was crawling over him. He raised his head and peered out from beneath the brim of his Stetson.

He could see nothing but he had the strange sensation that whatever it was had stopped.

He looked down the length of his body, saw his dust-covered boots sticking out of the end of his shelter, saw the glare of the sun reflected back by the almost-white sand.

There was nothing on his stomach or legs and his chest was clear. He looked at his right hand, nothing. Moving his head. he looked down at his left hand lying by his side, palm up.

Nestled quite comfortably in the palm of that hand sat a black scorpion.

His head fell back to the ground of its own accord. The sweat, which had been trickling out with the noon-day heat, now began to pour down his face. He felt it run into his ears and drip off his lobes.

Whatever happened in the next two minutes, he thought, had better happen quickly. The pain in his chest had reached new heights of agony. His breath whistled, but the whistling sound didn't come from his mouth or nose. It came from much, much deeper down.

Ignoring his chest, Henry John braced himself to move quickly. He'd seen before, as a child, when fear is an unknown quantity, how fast scorpions could tail-sting strike.

He remembered the scorpions he'd trapped as a boy with his friends, surrounding them with stones and stopping their escape with twigs held in pudgy fingers, watched as eventually, the scorpions turned on each other in a ritualistic dance of death.

Keeping his left hand and arm still, he raised his head and pushed himself up so that he rested on his left elbow. He could see the eyes of the scorpion looking at him, staring him out, waiting for him to try and move. It became a battle of wills.

Taking a deep breath through his nose, he coughed as the oxygen hit his lungs. The noise was enough to wake the dead. The scorpion sat, and Henry John saw the creature smile at him, daring him to move.

They faced each other like two gunslingers, each waiting for the other to make the first move.

Henry John looked at the gap in the front of the sailcloth. He didn't want to make a sudden move, flick the scorpion off only for it to land back on him via the sailcloth. On the other hand, he didn't want to get tangled up in the material, panic could set in, he might even roll on the scorpion, stinging himself to death in his bid to escape.

In his mind's eye, he pictured his movements. Saw himself fly forwards, the scorpion landing to his left as he darted towards the open sky.

No sooner had he thought it than he did it. The only thing he didn't count on was hitting the stick he'd used as a tent pole to keep the sailcloth up.

Scrambling out onto the hot sand, he turned and watched as the billowing sailcloth gently landed flat on the ground.

He could see no movement.

He waited.

Still nothing moved. He hadn't killed the scorpion, of that he was certain. Panic stricken he looked down at his left hand. It was empty.

He was loath to leave the sailcloth, it was too useful to him. Grabbing two corners, he flicked it into the air. If the scorpion was tangled up in it, this would free it.

It did. But not in a way that he could have imagined. The scorpion flew through the air and landed on the back of his horse. The horse bolted.

Helplessly, Henry John watched as his animal careened left and right, trying to shake off the creature on its back.

The horse disappeared over a crest in the sand. Henry John just stood and watched the empty space.

He folded up the sailcloth and kicked out the fire. Luckily, he still had a saddle-bag and canteen. The coffee pot had enough for a cupful, so he drank that and packed the pot, the mug and the plate he'd used, into the saddle-bag. Making sure he'd forgotten nothing, he flung the saddle-bag over his shoulder and began to walk.

The going was tough. The sand was soft and deep and each step made him sweat even harder. Pretty soon he was soaked through, and his legs were aching with the effort of putting one foot in front of the other.

He reached the crest of the dune where his horse had disappeared minutes before and scanned the horizon. Come on boy, he said to himself, you can make it, you can make it.

Then he saw the black lump on the sand. The head was moving slightly, the tail fluttered. The legs were still.

Henry John ran as fast as the loose surface would allow, falling frequently as his legs sank almost thigh-high into the soft, unrelenting sand.

He stopped short of the animal. He could see the whites of the mare's eyes staring at him in a resigned way. The scorpion had struck.

Henry John took out his gun and checked the desert floor around the animal to see if the scorpion was still there, but it was long gone.

His horse whinnied, saying don't worry, it wasn't your fault. He raised the gun and pointed it at the animal's head. He closed his eyes and squeezed the trigger.

There was no point in trying to carry the saddle. Henry John thought about it long and hard. The saddle was damn near as old as the horse.

He remembered the day he'd bought the horse and saddle. Tears jerked unwillingly from his eyes. It had taken a couple of weeks for horse and man to get used to each other.

He remembered the sores on his backside and

thighs as the hard saddle took its toll on his skin. The chaffing had lasted for well over a month. He'd used padding inside his jeans to ease the pain, but had been determined to break both horse and saddle.

He took the other saddle-bag and the spade. He began to shovel sand over the dead horse. The saddle he buried separately. Looking up, he stared past the sun, feeling its heat penetrate his eyeballs. But then he noticed something he hadn't noticed before. There was a tang in the air he didn't recognize.

The air, although hot and raw, was slightly moist. Years of living under the stars had tuned his nose in to extraordinary sensitivity.

The tangy smell was coming from due west, the direction in which he was travelling. The ocean. It had to be the ocean.

A new sense of purpose filled Henry John as he began his journey afoot. He didn't notice the sand trying to suck his boots off, or the blazing sun making the sweat evaporate almost as soon as it broke free of his skin. All he noticed was the smell.

He walked for the rest of that day. The sun ahead had lost its brilliant yellow, almost white visage and was now a deep, blood-red as it started to sink below the horizon.

Ahead, there was a hill. Too small to be called a

mountain, too big, Henry John thought, to be merely a hill. It would need a fresh day to scale that peak. He knew that. He was tired, too tired to continue. His chest reminded him of the pain he'd felt earlier in the day and his breath became laboured once more.

Time to stop.

All his instincts told him to travel when the sun went down, not during the heat of the day. But he couldn't go on any further.

Unfolding the sailcloth, he found another stick and set up camp. His bedroll took the hardness out the ground and, without even bothering to light a fire, he sipped a mouthful of water and lay back under the shelter. Within seconds, he was in a deep, dreamless, sleep.

Sun up. The new day broke in a cacophony of sound. High above him he saw the reason for the unfamiliar noise.

White birds, not as large as vultures, were circling in the early morning air. He'd no idea what sort they were, but they didn't seem to be circling him.

He remembered the scorpion, and before moving, he checked himself over. Nothing.

Henry John crawled slowly out of the shelter on arms and legs that hurt from the previous day's exertions. Standing, he stretched as best he could, feeling joints click as he did so. He stumbled around gathering up loose kindling and firewood. Already he could imagine the smell of the coffee which was still relatively fresh.

The fire lit, the coffee brewing, his aches and pains reduced, Henry John felt ready for the day.

The sun was just over the horizon, as blood-red coming up as it had been going down. He watched the shadows dance as the sun rose higher and higher. Gradually, the shadows disappeared and the red glow turned yellow and, finally, white.

The sweat began its daily trickle, the cold night air warmed up, and Henry John knew that soon, the full force of the sun would be upon him.

He doused the fire and packed up his kit, this time he was a bit more discerning about what he would take and what he would leave behind. He had no idea how much further the desert stretched, or indeed how much longer it would take to reach the ocean, but he did know he couldn't carry as much as he had the previous day.

The rifle and both saddle-bags, along with food and coffee, the canteen and the sailcloth and lariat. That was it, everything else was left behind.

It didn't feel any easier or lighter, but Henry John set off once more. The climb ahead looked daunting, and he wondered whether he'd make it.

The gentle slope was relatively easy, his thighs

screamed at him, but he coped. The ridge would not prove to be as easy. Using the rope, he tied everything to it and began to climb, dragging it all behind him from a loop on his belt.

Halfway up the crumbling bluff, the pain in Henry John's chest returned. The muscles in his arms contracted and his fingers went numb. He stayed where he was, fighting for breath and clinging on for dear life.

Below him some thirty feet, he looked at the sandy floor, strewn with sandstone outcrops and knew that if he fell, he'd die.

In through the nose, out through the mouth. He remembered. In and out, in and out, he tried to calm himself down and breathe normally.

His feet sent a cascade of debris falling to the ground; he saw himself following.

As quickly as it had started, the pain subsided and his breathing became regular again. Feeling returned to his fingers and his biceps unlocked. Picking his way carefully, he made his way to the top.

He stayed spread-eagled on the ground, panting, relaxing his muscles and flexing his fingers. Eyes shut tight.

Sitting up, he started to pull the rope. He heard the coffee pot and mug and plate clanging together as the saddle-bags hit the bluff, then they appeared over the edge and into safety.

He breathed a long, grateful, sigh of relief.

Henry John sat there for five more minutes. He felt the worst was over now. What came up, must come down. Standing, he turned. The sight fair took his breath away again.

No more than half a mile in the distance, the desert melted into water. Great, white, rolling, clouds of foaming water.

The ocean.

Tears sprang to his eyes. For as far as he could see, the ocean ebbed and flowed. The white birds he'd seen earlier were gently floating outside the cruel crash of the waves. He watched in awe.

A new strength filled him and he began walking. It took him thirty minutes to reach the shore line. The noise of the crashing waves was deafening, followed by a rustle as the water ebbed, dragging at the shore line and rattling the loose sand and stones together.

He dropped his saddle-bags and removed his leather boots and walked forward. He felt the power of the water as it swilled around his ankles, washing the sand from between his feet. He walked further out. The water pulled at his thighs and he almost lost his balance.

Bending down, he scooped up a hand full of the cold water and splashed it over his face, then he took his Stetson off and filled it to the brim.

The salt taste lingered in his mouth, it was unexpected. For some reason, the salt in the sea surprised him.

Refreshed, Henry John paddled back to the beach. Although he'd swum as a kid in ponds, he wasn't about to try it in this rough water.

He flopped down beside his saddle-bags and let the sun dry him off.

After a short nap, which again to Henry John's surprise, was dreamless, he took out the Wanted poster once more and studied the man's face. It felt eerily familiar, but Henry John knew he'd never seen this man before.

When he had memorized the face, he closed his eyes and saw it, printed there in his mind's eye. He was ready.

Taking a dime out of his vest pocket he tossed it in the air. Heads. He turned left and headed south along the shoreline.

Again, he walked for the rest of the day. It didn't feel as hot here next to the ocean, with the cool breeze blowing inland, the walk was a pleasure. The sea-salt air even seemed to do his lungs some good. As for the rest of that day, he had no trouble breathing whatsoever.

The sun began to sink, a sight he'd seen a thousand times before. But this time it was different. He stood and watched, mouth open in wonder, as the sun sank into the ocean.

The millions of ripples reflected red; it was as if the very water itself was on fire. The huge orb sank majestically from sight and warm, friendly water turned icy black and cold. A new dimension was added to his scant knowledge of the ocean.

He walked on for three hours, marvelling at the way the moon's rays reflected off the ocean. The black of the water was now silver as the moon rose. The water looked warm and friendly once more.

He halted by a large sand dune and set up camp. There was plenty of driftwood on the beach and in only a few minutes, he had a roaring blaze going.

Finishing off the coffee, he washed pot and mug and plate in the sea and set the shelter up. He stoked up the fire and crawled under the sailcloth onto his bedroll.

The moon was full, and he could plainly see the craters. Stars in their thousands twinkled back at him and the roar of the fire, with embers rising in the thermal, created a picture he'd never forget.

Sleep came, and with it the flickering dreams. He'd been over-confident. Assuming that, as he hadn't dreamt for the last two sessions, he'd get away with it now. He didn't.

Only these weren't dreams. These were night-marish images that flashed before him now. His mother's deathbed, the woman and child he'd found on the Plains, all the dead people he'd ever come across in his life were there in plain view.

Lastly, his wives.

They took it in turn to appear, arms out-stretched. Beckoning. He could hear their voices calling him.

His chest was on fire. As he breathed, it gurgled as if his lungs were full of water – or blood.

He was choking! Henry John was choking to death in his own nightmare and he couldn't do a damn thing about it.

His body was wet with the exertion of breathing the water – or blood was lapping round his neck, engulfing him.

He woke up. The sea was all around him. Not the cruel crashing waves of the evening before, but a gentle ripple of salt water, just rushing up the shore-line to wet him and then retreat.

The tide was coming in.

In a state of blind panic and with his lungs fit to burst, Henry John gathered up his soaked posses-sions and climbed atop the dune.

The camp fire was sizzling, soon to go out, and from where he stood he could see that the ocean had crept up the beach to get him. It must have moved over a hundred yards. He was lucky he woke up when he did.

Wet and cold, he wrapped himself up in the

damp bedroll and this time, slept undisturbed.

From the desert behind him the sun rose and warmed his bones and cramped muscles. Again, it took Henry John some minutes before he realized where he was and what he was doing.

He'd been stiff before, but not this stiff. It was as if the salt in the sea had dried up all over him and sealed him in its crust.

With aching fingers, he gathered driftwood together and built a roaring blaze again and began to warm himself up. There was just enough water left in the canteen for a fresh brew of coffee.

Warming up from the inside now, he felt better. He sat by the fire and gathered himself together. Heading south on the toss of a coin may not have seemed to be the best of planned journeys, but he didn't know the area at all so it was as good a way as any.

He packed up and set off again, the heat now building up, but the breeze kept him cool.

In the distance and slightly inland, he saw smoke. It could be a town or it could be a camp site. He decided to travel light and stashed his saddle-bags where he could find them and went on, holding just the rifle.

The smoke turned out to be coming from a variety of sources. It was a small township, no more than ten or twelve buildings. A ramshackle affair with no boardwalks and very little evidence that anyone did anything to keep the place tidy.

He walked straight down the middle of the street, the only street, and felt eyes on him.

There was a saloon; he would've been surprised if there wasn't. He walked in.

Even at this early time of the day, the saloon had six or seven people in it, all of whom were drinking red-eye.

A silence fell as Henry John approached the bar. He dropped a dime on the counter and the 'keep filled a whiskey tumbler to overflowing.

Without question, Henry John downed the liquid and coughed until he felt his insides were about to come out through his mouth.

''Fects most people that way, first time,' the 'keep said.

The man's voice was music to Henry John's ears as he suddenly realized he'd not heard the sound of a human voice for twelve days.

'Shoot me again,' Henry John said.

The barkeep filled the tumbler and this time Henry John sipped it down. The effect was better, the burning liquid entered his stomach and a warm glow spread throughout his entire body. He relaxed.

The general hubbub, of which there had been precious little, resumed. The other customers now took no notice of him at all.

103

Placing another dime on the counter, he picked the replenished tumbler up and leant on the bar, surveying the room. He was about to raise the glass to his lips when he caught sight of a man seated on his own in the corner.

Trying not to stare in the gloomy light, Henry John knew that face, and couldn't believe his luck.

Black Jake sat there for all the world to see. Henry John downed the whiskey and asked if there was board and lodging in the town.

The barkeep informed him that he had two rooms out back that he rented off, fifty cents, in advance.

Henry John threw the money on the counter and the 'keep led the way through to back of the saloon.

Black Jake looked up as he passed. Henry John nodded and the large man tilted his head so slightly, you wouldn't even know it.

Once in his room, Henry John checked the rifle; it was still loaded. He made his way back to where he'd buried his gear and brought it back to his room. He took out the Wanted poster and studied it. There was no mistake. The man in the saloon was Black Jake, and the poster said Dead or Alive!

CHAPTER FOUR

Henry John started to tremble. It was all very well saying you wanted to be a bounty hunter, in broad daylight, in a sheriff's office, in a large town like Red Rock. It was another thing to actually *become* one in a two-bit no-name town like the one he now found himself in.

Sure, he thought, I've used a gun before, I've killed people, but never out of choice. I've never gone out looking for a fight.

He sat on his bunk and slowly polished his handgun. The Colt Frontiersman was a faithful weapon, accurate and reliable. Nevertheless, he wanted to make absolutely sure. Besides, it gave him time to think.

He carefully cleaned each of the six chambers, cleaned out the barrel and peered through it, blowing it out from both ends. Satisfied, he reloaded it. It felt reassuring.

Next, he picked up the Winchester. The stock was battered and scarred, but the metalwork was in good order. Again, he unloaded it and cleaned all the moving parts as well as polishing up the barrel. Reloading it, be even inspected the bullets – just to be on the safe side.

He leaned the Winchester up against the wall and relaxed on the bed. He didn't figure on getting into the bed, by the smell of it, the sheets and blankets had never seen soap and water.

He rolled a cigarette. Despite his chest, he needed to calm his nerves. He lit up and drew deeply, the bitter tobacco made him cough and he couldn't finish the cigarette.

Now he needed a drink, his throat was red-raw. But Black Jake was in the saloon and he didn't know whether he could face that yet.

Sooner or later I've got to, he thought. Might as well be sooner. He got up and put his Stetson on, noticing how battered and misshapen it now was. Maybe he'd buy a new one when he got some money in.

He left the room, leaving the oil-lamp on low. The saloon had the same people in it as an hour ago. Jake still sat morosely at the table, the red-eye still in front of him.

Henry John went through his pockets and gathered the loose coins together. His folding money, what there was of it, was in his left boot – out of harm or temptation's way.

He asked for, and got, a full bottle and one glass which he took to a table near the door and poured himself a drink. He sipped it until his throat and stomach got used to it. The second one he downed, and the third and the fourth. It was then he realized he was hungry.

He walked back to the barkeep and asked if there was a cafe nearby. The barkeep laughed, too loud and too long.

'Nope, we ain't got no café. I can rustle you up some chilli though, always keep a mess of it bubblin' away.'

'Bowl o' chilli 'll do fine,' Henry John said, although he doubted his stomach would agree with him.

It took the barkeep two minutes flat to reappear with a steaming bowl of the most foul-looking meal Henry John had seen for a long time. When the barkeep said he kept a mess of it, he wasn't kidding, thought Henry John.

Hunger, though, was a slave driver, so, picking up the greasy spoon, he began to eat.

The fiery chilli was as hot as all hell, and pretty soon Henry John's tongue was on fire. The whiskey was no help at all. He rushed to the bar and in a voice that he didn't recognize as his own, asked for water.

The barkeep smiled. He'd been waiting for the request and already had a jug filled and glass standing by.

Henry John drank the tall glass of water in one go. The sweat was pouring down his face as the chilli got to work, and although the water cooled his mouth while he was drinking, as soon as he'd finished, the burning started all over again – if anything, worse than before!

The barkeep had a stupid grin on his face. He'd known how hot the chilli was and it was one of his major sources of entertainment, watching his customers suffer.

The rest of the saloon had their attention focused on Henry John as well – including Black Jake, who was himself eating a bowl of chilli with no side-effects at all, not even a sweat.

Now Henry John had a sense of humour, but with his mouth and stomach on fire with the chilli peppers, he failed to see the fun.

He grabbed the pitcher and glass and stormed back to his table where he proceeded to drink the entire pitcher full.

Black Jake watched the man carefully. His senses told him to keep an eye on this man. He didn't look like the usual saddle-bum that populated this town on and off.

Jake had used the saloon many times before, as had a lot of outlaws. There was no law here and nobody asked any questions. Once or twice Jake had caught the man eyeballing him. That put his hackles up. He continued with his chilli, which didn't have the same amount of peppers in it that Henry John's did. The barkeep knew better than that.

Henry John had finished trying to eat anything. His tongue gradually ceased its burning, his stomach, however, had not. He downed a couple more slugs of whiskey and began to feel more human.

He looked up and caught Black Jake staring at him. He looked away, pretending to gaze through the bat-wing doors. He picked up his whiskey glass and, as he drank, cast his eyes in Jake's direction once more. The man was still looking at him. His black eyes were penetrating, almost as if he was reading Henry John's mind.

It was obviously a stand-off, a trial of wills that Henry John couldn't afford to lose.

The coincidence of finding Black Jake – if that indeed was what it was – Henry John thought it was more like his own destiny, his fate – was too good to be true.

Having drunk enough for one night, Henry John decided it was time for bed. He picked up the half-empty bottle, put the glass in his vest pocket and walked across the saloon to the back door. Black Jake stood.

The man was a giant. Not just tall, indeed, he was even taller than Henry John's six-foot five frame, but he was big all over.

His enormous gut hung over both his belt and gun-belt, the shirt buttons so taut on the material, it seemed that they might snap off at any minute.

The face, large, round and red, was covered in a massive, black beard, that Henry John thought contained remnants of at least his last six meals.

But it was the eyes. Black, satanic pools of hatred, that glowered at Henry John. Malevolence seemed to ooze from every pore on the man's body.

Henry John continued his walk across the saloon, trying as best he could to avoid eye-contact with the big man.

He almost succeeded.

As he got to the end of the bar, he had to pass Black Jake's table. The big man stepped out in front of him.

'You ain't finished your chilli, mister,' he spat at Henry John.

He could smell the man, a sour, sickly, unwashed smell that was matched only by the man's fetid breath. He was a creature straight from hell.

'I've eaten all I'm gonna,' Henry John said and tried to get past, but the big man didn't budge an inch.

'I said, you ain't finished your chilli.'

This now came out not as a statement, but as an order.

Henry John looked straight at the man. In a fist-fight, Henry John knew he'd stand no chance. In a gunfight? He wondered about that, he wasn't too sure.

'An' I said I've eaten my fill.'

'Well, we don't think so, do we boys?' Jake looked around the saloon. The men seated at tables and trying not to get involved, merely grunted their replies. It was good enough for Black Jake.

Henry John had a choice: he either fought the man here and now, or he went back to the table and finished his chilli.

The chilli came second.

Backing off, Henry John made as if to return to his table. About ten feet away from Black Jake he stopped and turned around. Placing the whiskey bottle on the nearest table, he spread his feet, and let his arms hang loose.

'Maybe you'd like to finish the chilli,' he said. Even as he said it, the ridiculousness of the con-frontation hit him. Was he really going into a gunfight with a suspected bank robber, killer and rapist? All because the chilli was too hot? He must be mad.

But it was too late to back down. If he didn't make a stand, he'd be dead before sun up.

Black Jake ambled forward on his huge legs and stood within six feet of Henry John. He too spread his feet and his enormous arms hung by his side.

This was the signal the rest of the assembled company had been waiting for. Chairs were knocked over in their haste to be somewhere else right now. The barkeep took down a few bottles of whiskey from the shelf behind the bar, then unhooked the mirror and ducked down behind the counter.

'Your play, stranger,' Black Jake said.

Henry John was more relaxed than he ever thought he could be. In his mind, he saw the two of them draw, and he saw Black Jake hit the wooden floorboards with a crash that sent splinters into the air.

A grin appeared on the face of Henry John. Black Jake wasn't expecting that. Most of the fights he'd got into, his enemies were often intimidated by his sheer bulk, but this man was different. A puzzled frown appeared on his face as he pierced Henry John with his eyes.

The band tightened on Henry John's chest. Oh,

God, he thought, not now. Please, not now!

In that instant, both men drew simultaneously. Both weapons erupted in smoke and flame and the saloon reverberated with the explosions of the shells as they left the side-irons. Henry John was convinced that he could see the slug heading for his belly, but it missed. He was still standing.

So was Black Jake.

Silence.

Both men, with guns levelled, stood their ground. Not only could Henry John not believe the big man had missed him, he couldn't believe that he'd missed Black Jake.

He hadn't.

A stain appeared on the big man's shirt. It spread from his chest and ran down the outside of his clothes and dripped on the floor. A normal man would have been blown off his feet at this distance, maybe sent crashing through the counter.

In slow motion, Black Jake toppled forward and landed with a wood-splintering crash on the floor.

He was dead.

It then seemed that every nerve in Henry John's body woke up. His hand was shaking uncontrollably; it was an effort to re-holster his Colt.

His breathing, so shallow, was making him dizzy and the pain in his chest made him look down to make sure he hadn't been hit.

Henry John swayed on his feet.

The barkeep's head appeared over the top of the counter, eyes wide, scanning the scene.

'You done?' he asked.

'Yeah. I'm done. So's he.' Henry John pointed to the floor and the huge, dead frame of Black Jake.

'You know who he is – was – don't ya?' the barkeep said.

'Yeah, I know,' Henry John said.

'Then you know he's got a gang, an' they'll be here come sun-up.'

'Shit. No, I didn't know that,' Henry John said.

'If I was you, which I ain't, but if I was, I wouldn't hang around here for too long.'

'I better inform the sheriff,' Henry John said.

'We ain't got no sheriff,' the barkeep replied.

'Undertaker?'

'Nope.'

'Shit. What about the body?'

'We'll bury it later.'

'Was a fair fight,' Henry John added.

'Sure was. Don't make no difference no way anyhow. He's had that comin' for a long time. Evil bastard!'

'You check his room out, take what you want, I'll take care o' the rest. Ma fee for the funeral.'

'Fair enough.'

Henry John went to the back of the saloon as the

other paying customers returned. They all looked down at the dead man, then resumed their drinks and conversation as if nothing had happened.

In Black Jake's room, Henry John found money in the saddle-bags. More money than he'd ever seen. And a pair of matching pistols. Silver, with pearl handles.

Henry John grabbed them and most of the money, he left some for the barkeep. Then he high-tailed it out of the room, gathered his own stuff up and walked back into the saloon.

No one paid him any attention. He told the barkeep to keep what he found, then asked where Jake's horse was.

'The stallion outside,' the barkeep said. 'He ain't even fed him yet.'

'Thanks.' Henry John tipped his battered Stetson and left the saloon.

'See you around,' the barkeep shouted after him and then he, too, went to Black Jake's room. No sense in leaving valuables lying around for others to steal, he thought to himself.

The horse was massive, at least sixteen hands as would befit a massive rider. He walked the animal over to a trough and let it drink, then he got hay from the sorry-looking livery stable opposite and fed it to the horse, talking to the animal and stroking his head at the same time.

Within ten minutes, the horse missed Jake about as much as everybody else would and accepted his new master without question.

Climbing on to the saddle, Henry John took a final look around the town. It was dark, deserted. Except for the saloon, no lights showed. He walked the animal out of town, wondering how he should claim his reward.

Was it worth going back to Red Rock? With the money and possessions he'd acquired, he thought not.

The tide was high, the beach he'd walked along was now covered almost to the dune cliffs. He stopped the animal and gazed at the sea, mesmerised by the gently lapping waves as they caressed the sand.

He'd have to find somewhere to spend the night. That was his most pressing thought now, as his breath again came in laboured gulps.

The coastline along southern California seemed to be littered with small, out of the way, nameless townships, and it didn't take Henry John long to find a room for the night.

He kept away from chilli, however.

Checking into a small hotel-cum-saloon, Henry John counted up the cash he'd found in Black Jake's saddle-bag. It was a fortune, over one thousand and seven hundred dollars!

For some reason Henry John couldn't quite comprehend, he made up his mind to send one-thousand five-hundred dollars of the money to Sean Hollander. He hadn't thought of the boy in ten long years and hoped that Ben and Rose hadn't moved.

He spent nearly an hour writing, as best he could, a note to the boy.

Deer Shawn

I no you dont noed me, but I was the fell whod done brung you down to Rose and Bens place. i was with yur dady when he got kilt, but belive me boy we sure did git the fellas that kilt yur mom and bruther.

i bin doin bounty huntin, an thats where i got this money from.

you use it to git yurself a proper edukashun and dont you live like i done, i wish you and Rose and Ben well.

William Henry John

Henry John read the letter over and over He couldn't think of anything more to put in it, so he fashioned an envelope and addressed it care of the sheriff's office. That way he thought they'd get it. All he had to do now was find a stage-depot and get it off. That he'd do tomorrow.

There wasn't a soul in the saloon. Admittedly it was late, but nevertheless, he was surprised. The barkeep told him he had stew and bread on offer that night and Henry John accepted it gratefully.

The stew was delicious and Henry John washed it down with the coolest beer he'd tasted in a long time.

The saloon doors burst open and three cowboys walked in. They headed straight for the bar and ordered whiskey. Then they quizzed the barkeep about strangers in town. The barkeep eyed Henry John but didn't mention him.

The cowboys walked over to Henry John and asked him if he'd seen any strangers in town that night. Henry John shook his head.

'Can't say I have, mister,' Henry John said. 'Who you lookin' for?'

'A killer!' the cowboy replied.

'Oh, yeah. Who'd he kill?' Henry John asked.

'Our boss. Man known as Black Jake.'

'Ain't never heard o' him,' Henry John said, and downed the last of his beer.

The cowboys drank up and left.

Henry John took his bowl and glass to the counter and ordered another beer.

'Have one yourself,' he said to the barkeep.

'What for?'

'Because I'm payin' an' because you didn't mention me to them cowboys.'

'You who they're lookin' for?'

'I reckon so.'

'I'll have a beer,' the barkeep said, and poured two glasses from the pitcher.

The two men downed their beers and Henry John said goodnight.

Henry John relaxed on his bed, staring at the ceiling. He'd stuffed the envelope with the letter and money in it under the mattress, he just hoped he wouldn't forget it in the morning.

Sleep came quickly. So did the dreams.

This time the images were slow moving. He was running through a field of corn, he was a boy. He could tell that because the corn towered over his head.

The clear, blue sky overhead and the bright sunshine were all he could see through the maze of cornstalks. He was being chased. Not by anyone wanting to harm him. On the contrary, it was a small girl.

He was running through the cornfield with Sadie Mathews running after him. She wanted a kiss and he didn't want to give her one.

He smiled in his sleep as he remembered.

The rain came down. He was up a tree and couldn't get down. The trunk and branches were slippery and he was losing his grip.

Lightning followed the thunder and his fear of falling was equally matched by his fear of the lightning.

His father was under the tree, holding his arms in the air and telling Henry John to jump.

He did.

He was back in the rodeo ring, flat on his back, the calf had thrown him again. All the wind had been knocked out of him. He couldn't breathe. His head was going dizzy and he could see stars, if he didn't look at them directly.

He was going to faint, but his father pulled him upright by the shoulders and slapped his face. The pain on his flushed cheek made him breathe again.

Henry John opened his eyes. The oil-lamp was still burning and he was still on his bed, bathed in sweat.

The pain in his chest was intense again. The harder he tried to breathe the worse it became.

He heard voices.

Henry John wasn't sure if he *heard* voices, or whether he was *dreaming* voices. His eyes were open, so he figured he must have heard them.

He heard a gun hammer being cocked. It seemed to come from right outside his door.

Reaching over, he selected the two silver and pearl Colts, and waited.

Reality exploded in on him like a thunderbolt. The three cowboys.

They'd obviously asked around town and now

they'd come for him. He heard a twig snap outside the bedroom window; they'd split up.

Swinging his legs off the bed, Henry John crawled to the corner of the room that was opposite both door and window.

He stayed, braced against the wooden wall for what seemed like ages, before the door burst open and two men entered, firing as they came.

The shots landed harmlessly in the bed. In two shots, one from each gun, Henry John killed both men. He waited for the third.

From where he stood, he knew the man wouldn't be able to see him, so he kept very still.

He heard a voice calling out, and Henry John whispered a quiet, 'Yeah.'

The window opened and a rifle barrel was poked through, followed by the head and shoulders of the third man. Just as he realized that his two partners had been shot, and lifted his eyes from their bodies, Henry John shot again.

The slug took the top of the man's head off. There was no doubt he was dead.

Sweat was coursing its way down Henry John's face. He kept the guns out and levelled, in case.

No one else came gunning for him.

The barkeep called down the hall and Henry John answered him.

'It weren't me, mister,' the barkeep said.

'Makes no difference,' Henry John said. 'They'd've found me sooner or later.'

'Looks like you could use a beer.'

'Sure could.' Henry John followed the barkeep back into the saloon. Three or four men were gathered round the bar and silence fell as Henry John walked in. He suddenly realized he was still holding the two Colts. He smiled and re-holstered them.

'Fancy shootin' there, mister,' the barkeep said.

Henry John downed his beer. He hoped no one in the room could see the shaking of his hands.

'Jus' luck, is all,' he replied.

'Don't think so,' the barkeep went on. 'Those fellas were Black Jake's gang. You got rid o' them as if they was nothin'.'

'Well, I sure hope I get the reward,' Henry John said.

The room fell silent.

'You ain't no bounty hunter or nothin', are you, mister?' one of the men at the bar asked.

Henry John felt the mood of the saloon change.

'Hell, no. Jus' got into a fight, is all.'

The mood changed back to one of friendliness.

'Reckon you'll wanna get over to Red Rock,' the barkeep said. 'Sheriff's office there'll see about the reward.'

'Well, I don't reckon on ridin' that aways,' Henry

122

John said.

'Stage comes through tomorrow,' a cowboy said.

'You could always send a note in. We all heard what you did, stranger.'

'Mighty good o' you, men. I think I'll do that.'

That night, Henry John wrote his second letter. This time it was to the sheriff of Red Rock claiming the reward but asking for it to be sent, along with the enclosed envelope, to Sean Hollander.

He took the letter into the saloon and the barkeep and cowboys signed it as witnesses.

Henry John was a bit dubious about parting with all that money, but unless he actually took it back himself, he had no alternative.

The barkeep promised to hand it over to the stage. He also said he'd take care of the bodies.

Henry John said he wanted none of their possessions, so the barkeep was welcome to their horses and whatever else they had, in payment for his trouble.

The smile on the barkeep's face was a mile wide.

Henry John spent a peaceful night. The dreams didn't disturb him at all and when he awoke next morning, he felt refreshed.

The barkeep had kept his word and the bodies had been moved over to the livery stable. From there, they'd be dumped over at their own Boot Hill with little ceremony.

At breakfast, he was treated as a hero. It seemed that Black Jake and his gang were feared in these parts and their demise was a cause for celebration.

The town itself, which had no name, was a prettier sight in the daylight. Although ramshackle, it had a certain charm that Henry John could appreciate. That, and the constant sound of the roaring ocean in the background, was somehow calming.

But he couldn't stay there. After all the backslapping was over and he'd finished his last cup of free coffee, Henry John made his farewells and slowly rode out of town.

He steered his horse back to the shoreline and dismounted. He wanted to be alone for a while and the beach offered him the solace he required.

He'd seen water before, although freshwater and only in ponds or lakes, but the sight of this massive expanse of water made him feel minute, insignificant. It was frightening.

The sun's rays reflected off the water. A golden glow shone on the surface and the white of the waves, as they crashed onto the sand and shingle sent a wave of good feeling through Henry John.

But again, he couldn't stay there long. He felt this compulsion to keep moving. Still heading south, he continued his journey, keeping the ocean in sight to his right and the hills and desert to his left; he felt as if he was riding down the dividing line of the world.

The breeze coming off the ocean took the direct heat of the sun away, but its rays still beat down remorselessly. In the desert, he saw the mirages and the shimmering heat haze.

The occasional lizard, mouth wide open in an attempt to keep its body temperature down, stood sentinel on a rock or stone, so still it appeared to be dead until the pink tongue slithered out of its mouth and back in again tasting the air.

The noon-day sun beat down, the heat rising from the sand and the glare from the water were all taking their toll on Henry John. He needed to sleep.

Ever aware now of snakes and scorpions, he chose his site carefully. He unpacked his faithful sailcloth and set it up, the bedroll he unfurled and placed in the shade of his makeshift tent. He lined rocks all around the outside of the sailcloth to keep out anything big enough to cause him grief.

Untying his gun belts, he placed them inside the tent. Then he unsaddled his horse and tethered the animal in the shade of the rocks, filled his Stetson with water and let the animal drink it.

It was quiet, peaceful and he looked forward to his sleep.

His chest began again. Just as he was entering his shelter, a stab of pain shot through him like a bullet. He collapsed to the ground, half in and half out of

125

the shelter, and there he stayed.

The room was full of smoke and the noise from the piano in the corner was thundering through his ears. He'd drunk too much whiskey and everything was spinning wildly. He blinked, then shut his eyes.

As he did so, he keeled over and hit the dirty wooden floor. On his way down he'd made a grab at the table, bringing that down with him. The whiskey and beer landed on top of him, soaking his back, but he didn't feel it.

He felt the boot hit his ribs, but no pain followed. Someone stood on his hand, but he didn't feel that either. He heard the shouting, the curses of the people whose drinks he'd spilled and card game he'd ruined.

Then they were laughing at him, pouring water over his head, not to wake him up, just to get a laugh. After all, he was the town drunk.

He felt the hands grab him sharply round his ankles and he was dragged across the floor. Broken glass dug into his back and scratched him. He was dragged through pools of liquid and cigarette and cigar butts and anything else that was on the floor.

He knew he was grinning. A drunken stupor had overtaken him, but he still grinned. Whiskey was poured down on his face. He managed to get some in his mouth, the rest stung his eyes. But he didn't feel it.

His head bumped into a chair, someone was still sitting on it and he saw the man's boot land within inches of his head.

Then he was outside, still being dragged. He felt the rough boardwalk, splinters of wood entered his rump, but they didn't hurt either.

Then he felt as if he was flying through the air. His back landed on the compacted dirt of the street, still, he was being dragged. Vaguely, he was aware of other people now. They were laughing and joking about something, but he didn't know what. He felt his shirt being ripped off and his trousers being pulled down, they got stuck on his boots so they were left around his ankles.

Other hands roughly grabbed him and he was lifted into the air. They were swinging him back and forth, back and forth, then he landed in the trough.

The shock of the cold water almost, but not quite, sobered him up. He grinned at the assembled company and closed his eyes.

He slept in the trough all night, up to his neck in the fetid water.

At sun-up, rough hands shook him, but these hands weren't laughing at him. These hands were pitying him. They shook him and shook him until he felt his head was going to come off.

Henry John awoke in his shelter. He was being

shaken and a gun was inches from his mouth. Henry John blinked.

The gun was still there, so was the leering Mexican face. He could see the black stubble on the man's chin and he could smell his sour body odour.

So, it wasn't a dream.

'Do not move a muscle, *señor*,' the man said. 'I should hate for this gun to go off accidentally.'

Henry John looked past the man to see if he was alone or had company.

He couldn't see anyone else.

Both the Colts were under the blanket behind Henry John's head. It would be too obvious, he thought.

The Mexican's handgun was inches from his face. His breathing became laboured again, in through the nose, out through the mouth. Beads of sweat ran down his face and landed on his shirt.

Henry John was panting like mad, his chest heaving. The Mexican didn't even notice.

'Now get out, *señor*, nice an' eezy, an' don't make no sudden movements.'

Henry John raised himself onto his elbows. His left hand, out of sight of the Mexican, rested on the sandy ground. He scooped sand into his palm and clenched his fist.

As Henry John moved forward, the Mexican

moved backwards, keeping the gun at arm's length and the barrel aimed at Henry John's face.

'I jus' want your money, *señor*, then I'll ride out of here. You don't have to worry.'

Henry John stared the man in the eyes without saying a word. He could see that the man was lying; there was no way Henry John was going to get out of this alive – unless—

He had to do something, and quickly. If only the pain in his chest would go away.

'Put your hands in the air,' the Mexican said.

As Henry John did so, he threw the sand with his left hand and knocked the gun sideways with his right. The Mexican yelled as the sand went in his eyes. Then he yelled some more when Henry John's fist busted his nose.

As the Mexican fell backwards, Henry John picked up the gun and pointed it at the stricken man who was trying to stop his nose from bleeding.

Before he could shoot, the Mexican was on him, splattering blood into Henry John's face as the man lunged forward, fighting for his life.

The two wrestled on the ground, rolling over and over, the gun in Henry John's right hand was ineffectual as the Mexican had a vice-like grip on Henry John's wrist.

Henry John brought his knee up into the man's groin. Eyes went skywards as the pain paralysed his muscles and he let go of Henry John's wrist and lay in the foetal position, clutching his privates.

The pain in Henry John's chest was almost making him see double, his breath, what there was of it, was coming in laboured pants. There was not enough oxygen in him to keep him standing much longer.

'Don't shoot, *señor*,' the man managed to say between clenched teeth.

From the look on Henry John's face, the Mex knew he was a dead man. He shouted for all he was worth. Too late, Henry John realized he was shouting for help from outside.

From behind a dune, two more Mexicans emerged brandishing handguns. Henry John shot the man with the busted nose and dived into his shelter.

Retrieving the Colts, he came out firing.

The second Mex went down, the third, seeing his *compadres* already dead, made a run for it.

Henry John took careful aim – then fired.

The Mex flew forward and landed in a heap of tangled arms and legs. He didn't move.

Checking the other two first, Henry John walked across and checked the third man. They were all dead.

So inured to death had he become that the first thing Henry John did was to check through his

Wanted posters to see if they had money on their heads.

To his major disappointment, they weren't among the posters.

He next checked out their horses, but there was nothing there that interested him. So he set them free to fend for themselves.

The three dead men he left where they lay. He couldn't see the point in burying them.

Gathering up his possessions, Henry John mounted his horse and headed south again, leaving the bodies for the buzzards.

With sudden realization, Henry John had become a killer.

As he rode south, he went over the killings of the three Mexicans. He had no remorse. He even remembered *not* thinking about what he was about to do. It didn't even occur to him not to kill them, it had become automatic.

What he needed now, he thought, was breakfast.

The ocean to his right had lost its magic. He hardly glanced at it any more. It had become as much of the scenery as the desert or the mountains. All Henry John was interested in was earning enough money to send back to Sean.

Another town loomed into view. This one was different. It was well kept, clean. To his left, outside town, he saw rolling plains. The desert had stopped its advance and the grass grew.

He could see the herd contentedly grazing. There must have been a thousand of them, he thought.

The sudden image of his second wife and children was so strong that for a moment, he thought they were standing in the pasture.

He removed his Stetson and smiled. The smile faded as the images disappeared. He hung his head, chin resting on his chest. Tears formed and attempted to run down his cheeks, but he blinked them back. He wasn't going to cry any more.

The smiling face of his wife looked up at him, and he smiled back.

Dismounting, Henry John led his horse into town. He felt the eyes of the townsfolk on him as he walked down the street, but no one caught his eye.

Both sides of the street had boardwalks and they were clean. The buildings were brightly painted and stained, windows clean. A whole variety of stores displayed their wares, from dress shops to hardware, a milliner's window was full of bonnets, the sort of bonnets he would have liked to buy his wife.

The hotel was painted a bright yellow, so bright it hurt his eyes as the sun reflected off it. The windows were adorned with flower boxes full of bright red and bright blue flowers that Henry John had never seen before.

Blue drapes framed the windows, and the red double-doors gleamed in the sunlight.

He tethered his animal to the hitching-post, that was also painted bright yellow. Henry John looked down at his dust-covered clothes and for once, was ashamed to be walking into a hotel in such a mess.

Looking around, he caught sight of the red, white and blue barber's pole. He walked across the street and entered the shop.

It too, was brightly decorated. The barber, a short man in his fifties, Henry John guessed, was standing on a wooden box, clipping someone's hair.

He stopped when Henry John entered, and smiled.

'Won't keep you a minute, stranger,' he said amicably.

'Thanks,' John Henry replied.

'Take a seat. There's a newspaper there if you want it.'

'Don't like to get the seat dirty,' Henry John said.

'Don't you worry, it's only dust, we'll soon have you looking spic and span.' The barber laughed and continued clipping.

Henry John sat on the padded seat that ran down the entire length of one wall. He picked up the newspaper and scanned through it. His reading wasn't all that good, but he knew enough to get the gist of the stories.

He looked at the pictures first, small advertisements showing brushes or guns or ploughs. On page three, there was an engraving of the town done by a local artist. It sure looked pretty, Henry John thought, and smiled into the newspaper.

'Plan on staying long, stranger?' the man who sat in the chair asked.

'Nope. Jus' passing through, I guess,' Henry John replied. 'Sure is a pretty town you got here.'

'Sure is, the prettiest and the best in southern California. We pride ourselves on that,' the man said.

The barber finished the man's hair and began to brush the floor. The man in the chair stood and left a silver dollar on the table, then put his hat on and, saying goodbye to both the barber and Henry John, he left.

'What can I do for you, mister?' the barber said.

'Shave, cut and a tub, if 'n you have one.'

'Sure have. Take a seat, I'll get the tub ready.'

Henry John sat in the ornate barber chair. He rested his head back on the soft leather and continued to read the paper.

The sound of shouting and people running along the boardwalk broke Henry John's concentration. Standing, he walked towards the window and looked out into the street.

Opposite the barbershop, the brick-built edifice

of prosperity, the Cattleman's Bank, stood in all its splendour.

He could see the sheriff, gun out, running towards it. Two men emerged from the bank door, both wearing bandannas to cover their faces. They were carrying money bags. Henry John knew the money was not theirs.

He put his Stetson on and opened the barber-shop door. People were running every which-way, trying to get to cover before the shooting started. The sheriff stood in the middle of the street as the robbers emerged, he raised his gun and loosed off a shot. It was wild, went nowhere near the two men, who steadied themselves and shot the sheriff where he stood.

Henry John stepped into the street. Cool. Concentrated. The two bank robbers were tying the money bags to the pommels of their saddles, confi-dent that no one else would challenge them in this pussy-foot town. They hadn't counted on Henry John being there.

'Hold it, right there,' he shouted.

The two men, still with handguns out, turned to see who'd done the shouting. They saw the tall man in the street and were so cock-sure, they finished tying on the money bags before turning around to face him.

Henry John stood his ground. His silver Colts

were still in their holsters.

The two men re-holstered their weapons and smiles appeared on their faces.

'Well, well, lookie-here,' one said to the other. 'We got ourselves a regular hero.'

Both men laughed. They'd seen enough towns and enough sheriffs in this backwater to know they were safe. The long arm of the law wasn't quite long enough for them.

The two bank robbers separated, putting at least ten feet between themselves, and they faced Henry John.

They looked the man over and thought he posed no threat to them. He looked just like what he was, a saddle-bum.

'Get smart, mister,' one of the men said.

'Yeah, get back to your chicken farm, or whatever it is you do,' the other man said and they both laughed.

'I can't see no chickens,' Henry John said in a deep voice that hushed the town. 'Less o' course I'm lookin' at two.'

The smiles left the faces of the two young men.

'What you say? You callin' us out, mister?'

'Seems to me you're already out, boy,' Henry John said.

The coolness of his voice and attitude made both men wary. They stepped further apart; the three men now formed a perfect triangle.

Simultaneously, the two men went for their guns. They were quick, but not quick enough.

Henry John had the two Colts out, levelled, cocked and firing long before the two bank robbers knew what hit them.

The town, which had gone deathly quiet before the shooting, was even quieter now. There was no movement. The bodies of the bank robbers lay in the dirt where they'd fallen.

Henry John walked across to them, guns still out and ready to shoot again.

He needn't have worried. Both men were dead.

Slowly, the townsfolk emerged. They stared at Henry John in wonder and fear, but they went straight to the sheriff first.

He was still alive. The bullet had lodged in his upper-left chest and he was hurt, but he was still breathing.

One of the men ran off to get the doc, another the undertaker. Henry John thought the tub might be ready now, so he turned and walked back to the barbershop.

The barber, all five-feet one inch of him, was standing open-mouthed as Henry John entered.

'That was just about the best bit o' shootin' I ever did see,' the man said.

Henry John sat back in the chair and waited for

his shave.

'Yessiree,' the man went on. 'It's a privilege to shave you, mister, a real privilege.'

Still Henry John said not a word.

The door burst open and three men entered. One, in a charcoal-grey suit, rushed straight up to Henry John and grabbed his hand and started pumping away as he babbled his gratitude.

Henry John realized that he was the bank manager, and when the man had dang-near shook his arm off, Henry John said, 'No problem.'

'No problem! Did you hear that, boys?' the bank manager said.

'Sure did.'

'Mister, that was the bravest thing I ever did see. You saved me a lot of embarrassment and the town a whole lot of grief. An' on behalf of the town council, I want to thank you most sincerely.'

Henry John nodded. 'You know who those men were?' he asked.

'Nope. We never seen 'em in these parts afore,' a man who turned out to be the mayor, answered.

He went on: 'Mister, for what you done today, the town is mighty grateful, if'n you decide to stay awhiles, everythin' is free. Hotel, saloon, hell, every-thin'.'

'Thank you kindly, mister,' Henry John said, 'but right now I'd like to get a shave, my hair cut and relax in a nice, hot tub.'

'God-dang,' one of the men said. Everyone was so excited they couldn't do enough for William Henry John.

CHAPTER FIVE

Sheriff Henry John dropped his cigar in the tub.

'Yep. Town council were unanimous,' the barber said.

'I'll have to think about that,' Henry John said.

'You still get the thousand dollars anyways.'

'That reward or bounty?'

'Reward from the bank.'

'Any Wanted posters out on those two?'

'Not that I know of, but then again, I'm jus' the barber.'

Henry John sat and pondered in the hot tub. He'd been riding the range for more than fifteen years. Maybe it was time to settle down. Hell, he didn't even know the name of this place, yet after the attempted bank robbery, they voted him in as sheriff!

The cigar had been replaced with another. Try as

he might, Henry John couldn't get the peace and quiet he craved. Every time he settled back in the tub, someone came in and congratulated him, or asked if there was anything he wanted, when all he wanted was to be left alone. He gave up.

He'd soaked in the tub for twenty-minutes, he'd been shaved and his hair had been cut and there, on the back of a chair, were the clothes he unpacked from the small case.

He towelled himself off quickly, in case someone else decided to visit, and got dressed.

Now he felt like a drink. The only drawback was, he wouldn't be able to have a quiet beer, he knew that.

He walked in through the bat-wing doors and the saloon erupted into spontaneous applause. Henry John had never been so embarrassed in his life. He blushed from head to toe and broke out into a sweat. Then his chest started up again.

He felt the tightness that heralded the shortness of breath. He heard the wheeze as he began to pant, his lungs whistled as he tried to fill them with the life preserving oxygen. Again, he was surprised that no one seemed to hear him pant or wheeze. They were all too busy slapping him on the back and offering to buy him drinks.

Henry John stayed for three beers. He would have liked more, but the attention was too much for him. These well-meaning folk were scaring the day-lights out of him. He wanted to tell them that being alone out on the range or the plains or the desert, a man got used to his own company. While he could tolerate a one-on-one, the people who thronged around him, trying to touch him or catch his eye, was just too much.

He made his excuses, thanked them for the hos-pitality and neighbourliness, fended off questions about being the next sheriff, and, eventually, managed to get outside.

His breathing became slightly better, the sweat began to slow down and the pain in his chest ebbed away to nothing.

He'd forgotten to check in at the hotel and he went back to the yellow-painted rail outside, but his horse was gone. Panic set in. All his possessions were on that animal; without it, he had nothing.

The large man with the leather apron settled his fears. The animal had been fed, watered and groomed and was now in a stall with fresh straw and was being well looked after.

Henry John thanked the man and entered the hotel. The clerk was seated behind the desk, wearing a suit and shirt and tie. He was the smartest clerk Henry John had ever met.

The man knew who he was and told him his room was ready, first floor, best room in the hotel. Then he told Henry John what a privilege it was for both he and the hotel to have him come stay there.

Henry John was again embarrassed, but thanked the man and quickly climbed the stairs.

What he needed now was peace and quiet and sleep. Stopping halfway up the carpeted staircase, he turned and said, 'Please don't let anyone up for at least two or three hours. I gotta get some shut-eye.'

'Sure thing, sir. You can rely on me. No one will disturb you.'

Henry John thanked the man and entered his room.

It was big. Too big for one person. Underneath the huge window opposite was the largest bed he'd ever seen. The room was fully carpeted, it had two wardrobes, three chests of drawers, two jugs and bowls, a desk and two armchairs.

Henry John whistled through his teeth. He'd never seen anything like this before.

He took his jacket off and hung it in the wardrobe. Then he removed his boots and lay down on the bed. There were small tables either side of the bed, each with an oil-lamp on top. The one nearest him also had a carefully-folded newspaper.

Idly he picked it up and slowly began to read through the lead stories.

One man's name caught his attention. It was the

name that prevented him becoming sheriff of this town, the name of which he still didn't know.

He formulated a plan. He'd leave the horse here and get a stagecoach to Flagstone, Arizona, where he'd pay a surprise call on the man he'd just read about. Then maybe, he'd return and settle down.

With a grin on his face, Henry John refolded the newspaper and put it back on the small table. Then he closed his eyes and—

He wouldn't let anyone else carry the coffins. He had to do it alone.

Before they unloaded his wife from the back of the black-plumed funeral cart, William Henry John lifted out the small, white casket. It was no more than two-and-a-half feet long and some eighteen inches wide. It was as light as a feather.

He carried it through the gates of the cemetery, past the line of people who'd turned up to pay their last respects, and then he returned for the next casket.

It too, was small, smaller even than the first. He fought to control his shaking, the hard lump at the base of his throat made it impossible to swallow. He kept his head low and carried this casket to the graveside.

He turned for the third and final time and, with the help of three neighbours, pulled out the last casket. That of his wife.

They walked slowly to the grave and gently lowered the casket onto the ropes that went across the hole that would be his family's final resting place for all eternity.

His only thought was that he wished he was with them.

The funeral service was a blur. He didn't hear a word the preacher said. He neither looked left, right or up. He stared at what was left of his life as one by one the three caskets were lowered into the grave.

He remembered people shaking his hand, he remembered the kisses of the women on his cheeks. He remembered the stinging of the salty-tears as they ran down his face silently.

His chest began to tighten. There was something wrong in there, he knew that. But for the life of him he didn't know what. Maybe he'd go see the doc. Yeah, that was it. He'd go see the doc.

Apparently, one his closest neighbours had arranged for everyone to come back to their house, tea, coffee, biscuits, nothing too elaborate. But Henry John rode home alone. He didn't want to see anyone. He didn't want to talk to anyone.

He needed a drink.

That drink, he remembered, lasted nearly six months.

He'd listen as people turned up at his homestead

and bang on the door – a door he never went to open. Some banged so hard it seemed that they'd break it down. Others tapped softly for a minute or two, then quietly left.

The banging continued, it became louder and louder and – Henry John opened his eyes. The ceiling was miles away, then it suddenly descended until he thought it would squash him flat like a bug.

Then it was where it should be.

Someone was banging on the door, gently, but insistently.

'It ain't locked,' he yelled.

The desk-clerk entered carrying a tray. On it was a coffee-pot, a cup and saucer, milk, sugar and a hot meal.

'Excuse me for knocking on your door, sir,' he said. 'But it has been four hours so I thought you might be thirsty and hungry.'

He placed the tray on the desk and added, 'Compliments of the hotel, sir.' He gave a slight bow and backed out of the room.

Henry John didn't even have time to register a thank you.

Thirty minutes later, belly full of the delicious stew and coffee, Henry John relaxed in one of the armchairs.

There was another knock on the door. He closed

his eyes and wished the person away, but that didn't work.

'Come on in, it ain't locked.'

The mayor stood, hat in hand on the threshold and Henry John stood up and walked across the room. The mayor held his hand out and Henry John shook it, feeling slightly awkward at all these pleasantries.

'I'm sorry to disturb you, Mister John, but I was wonderin' if you'd had time to think about staying here in Eldorado Town?'

'Eldorado?'

'Yes, sir, that's our town.'

'Eldorado, eh. I was wonderin'.'

The mayor coughed.

'Come on in,' Henry John said and closed the door. The two men sat in the leather armchairs.

'Room all right for you, is it?' the mayor asked.

'Finest room I ever did see,' Henry John replied.

There was an awkward silence.

Henry John stood and said, 'Look, I appreciate the offer, but there's something I have to do first. I have to get to Flagstone. After that, well, I jus' might want to settle here in Eldorado. Seems a right neighbourly town.'

'Is there anything we can help out on?' the mayor asked.

'No, no. It's jus' someone I have to see. Once.'

'Is there no way I can persuade you to stay?'

'No. I gotta do this. The only thing I'll say is that, once I've been to Flagstone, I'll come back. If'n the job is still open, I'll take it right gladly.'

'That's what I was hopin' you'd say.' The mayor stood up, smiled and held his hand out again. Henry John shook it.

'Any idea when the stagecoach leaves?' Henry John asked.

'Whenever you're ready to go. We'll lay on a stagecoach and driver and shotgun to take you to Flagstone. An' back again, if you wish.'

'Beginnin' to feel like the President,' Henry John said with a coy smile on his face.

'It's the least we can do,' the mayor said.

'Sun up OK?'

'No problem. I'll tell the desk clerk to have breakfast sent up.'

The mayor said his farewells and left.

Henry John sat in a stunned stupor. Hell, he thought, all I did was kill a couple of bank robbers.

Henry John decided the best thing to do was have a couple more beers, maybe in a quieter saloon, then an early night. He picked up the newspaper and re-read the story.

There was no mistake. It was the same name, same man. He smiled and put the paper down and went to find a saloon.

Every one he looked into was full to overflowing. Seemed as if the whole town was out celebrating. As soon as anyone caught sight of Henry John, he was gently manhandled inside and drinks were bought for him as he was asked to relay the story over and over again.

The 'early night' turned out to last until the small hours. He managed to crawl into bed and slept like a log.

The newspaper was curled up in his arms as he slept.

CHAPTER SIX

At sun-up there was a knock on his door and breakfast was served in bed – Henry John could get used to this. Eating up quickly, he dressed and readied himself for the two-day journey

There was another knock at the door. The mayor stood outside holding a brown parcel.

'I came to wish you well, Henry John,' he said. 'Also, my good lady wife noticed you weren't wearing a waistcoat and the Ladies' Circle clubbed together and asked me to present you with this.' He handed the parcel over to Henry John.

'Well, please thank the Ladies' Circle for their kindness,' Henry John said as he unwrapped the parcel.

Inside was a brilliant-red waistcoat. He held it up and smiled. 'That sure is a fine-looking garment,' he added.

'I look forward to your return,' the mayor said. 'The stagecoach is ready when you are.'

'I'm ready now,' Henry John said and put the waistcoat on. He then put on his guns and his jacket and finally, his new, black Stetson. He looked at himself in the mirror and was satisfied.

The stagecoach was surrounded by people who clapped and cheered as he left the hotel. The flush on Henry John's face matched the colour of his new waistcoat.

The stagecoach pulled out and the cheers rang in his ears. Henry John was the only passenger. On the leather seat opposite him was a wicker hamper and when he opened it he saw it was cram-packed with food, a bottle of whiskey and a sealed jug of beer. These people sure know how to look after a body, he thought.

The first day of the journey was uneventful and Henry John slept through most of it. The trail was relatively smooth and although the stagecoach was not exactly going hell-for-leather, the breeze through the side windows was enough to keep him relatively cool.

That night they arrived in Big Bear and to his amazement, the town of Eldorado had already sent a rider ahead to the hotel to let them know he was due in.

Although he was greeted by the hotel owner, who

turned out to be the brother of the mayor of Eldorado, he was relieved to find there was no congregation waiting for him.

The room – again, the best in the house – was ready for him as was a new, white shirt carefully laid out on the bed.

He put the shirt over a chair and, taking his jacket and boots off, he climbed on to the bed and closing his eyes, tried to relax.

Sleep came easily. It seemed to come too easily these days.

The images flashed again, flitting past so quickly they appeared only as blur. The face of the man stopped briefly, then flew off again. The same man he'd seen earlier; he recognized the black moustache.

There seemed to be a serenity there, he couldn't describe it, only that it was very peaceful and quiet. There was no anxiety.

It was this very quiet that filled him with foreboding. His breathing became laboured, sweat broke out on his forehead, he could see his own crimson chest rise and fall, rise and fall, as he attempted to fill his lungs. He felt as if he was drowning.

He awoke with a start. The sun was up, he'd slept all through the night. He changed into his new shirt and walked downstairs. The hotel owner was already in the dining room and he rose to greet Henry John.

'We left you to sleep. I hope we did the right thing, Mister John.'

'Thank you kindly, I sure needed that.'

'Breakfast?'

'That would be appreciated. Perhaps I could have the bill now, to save time.'

'That's been taken care of, sir.'

Henry John didn't argue.

The stagecoach left Big Bear and he resumed his journey. The scenery was totally different to what he had expected. Mountains and fir trees surrounded Big Bear, then as suddenly as they appeared, the desert spread out before them.

The day was long and tiresome. Henry John ate and drank well on the journey, the wicker basket having been replenished while he slept.

The driver, who so far had been quiet and not bothered Henry John at all, shouted out that they should be in Flagstone in two to three hours.

Henry John closed his eyes once more. This time he didn't sleep, he thought. The man he was about to visit had recently been appointed, and Henry John felt the butterflies in his stomach as the excitement built up inside him.

Would the man be pleased to see him? He hoped so.

He was rudely woken up by shouting and gun-shots. The stagecoach was careening wildly along the trail.

The shots were coming from the shotgun rider, the shouts from the driver.

'In'ians, Mr John. We're being attacked by In'ians!'

Henry John reached under his seat and pulled out the Winchester rifle. Leaning out through the window, he began to take as careful aim as he could and fired.

He watched as the Indian fell from his unsad-dled horse and hit the desert floor. Then he counted. There were only six of them, five now. Henry John kept up a steady volley of shots, four left, three, two.

He could hear the arrow heads hit the rear of the stagecoach, one managing to penetrate the wood and he had time to look at the barbed arrowhead hanging through.

There was a scream from above and the shotgun rider landed with a bone-crunching thump. Henry John knew he was dead, the two arrow shafts stick-ing out his body confirmed that.

The arrows were raining in thick and fast, he could hear their dull thud. He marvelled at how only two Indians could fire so many arrows so accu-rately while riding a galloping horse.

The arrows slowed down. The Indians were dropping back.

He continued firing, but the two remaining Indians had lost heart. He watched as they reined in their animals and stopped. They were watching him as he them.

The stagecoach lurched onwards, the team of four galloping for all they were worth.

In the distance, Henry John could make out the outlines of buildings. Flagstone.

He called out to the driver, but got no response. Either the man couldn't hear him over the noise of the wheels and horses, or—

The town loomed up and the stagecoach came to a halt.

The driver fell to the ground – dead.

Henry John opened his eyes. The room was bright – too bright – and he closed them again. In the near distance, he could hear muffled voices. He couldn't hear what they were saying, it was just a drone.

He could hardly breathe. The pain in his chest had almost disappeared, but he rasped. He could hear a gurgling sound, and he wondered where it was coming from.

He concentrated on breathing. In through the nose, out through the mouth. He smiled. No one saw it.

He opened his eyes once more, but still the light was too bright. He half closed them and peered out from beneath his eyelids. He actually saw his eyelashes. They stood out like tree-trunks. He'd never noticed that before.

There was a smell in the room that was vaguely familiar.

Clean. It smelled clean.

He still couldn't open his eyes wide enough to look around properly, but shapes appeared, blurred up against the brightness, but shapes that moved.

Henry John tried to turn his head, but the effort made him pant more. He closed his eyes and concentrated.

Then he realized his mouth was wide open in a silent scream. He felt the air burn down the back of his throat and then he knew where the gurgling sounds were coming from.

They were coming from him.

Panic set in. The sounds had never been this clear before. The numbness he felt all over his body had never been there before. What the hell was going on here?

He felt hands on his shoulders. He opened his eyes and the brightness had disappeared. In its place he saw a face. Black-hair, black-moustache, he'd seen that face before. But where?

He heard words, but he couldn't understand

156

them. He looked down at his body and saw the splash of crimson on his chest. The waistcoat, he thought.

But when he looked again, the red had spread. It pooled on either side of his body. He closed his eyes again.

He tried to move, but none of his limbs responded. He could feel nothing.

The voices started up again. Why the hell couldn't they speak clearly? He shouted out to them, but no sounds escaped his lips. His head was spinning and he couldn't stop it.

His eyes – wide open now – saw the man's face clearly. He recognized it but he didn't know the man, only that he'd seen that face.

Where? He didn't know.

The light was brighter, the man's head seemed to have a halo round it. Henry John's eyes widened still, he panted and tried to drag in air, the faster he breathed the less air he got.

Slowly, he turned his head to the left, his head was all he could feel. The rest of his body wore a cold-numbness that was relaxing in a strange way. He felt calm.

His eyes focused on the left side of the room. He saw a framed piece of paper on the wall, then another. There was a picture; Henry John vaguely recognized the group. But his brain refused to

157

enlighten him.

There was a large desk and leather-backed chair. The desk was tidy, papers piled up on the left and right, an inkwell and stand in the centre.

Then he saw the wooden sign on the desk. Light-coloured wood with gold lettering. He focused harder. He saw each of the characters in turn but they refused to turn into words:

SEAN HOLLANDER, MD

It should mean something, he thought, but for the life of him he couldn't think what.

He remembered the woman. He saw the flash and felt a dull thud.

William Henry John's eyes stopped seeing, the nameplate was printed there for eternity.

'He dead, Doc?'

'Yes. I'm afraid so.'

'He sure put up one hell of a fight, didn't he?'

'Took him four days to die,' the old doc said. 'Any normal man would have died instantly after taking two barrels at close range. Sadie Webster will hang for sure.'

'What the hell do you think he was mumbling about, Doc?'

'I guess we'll never know,' Doc Hollander leaned forward and closed the eyes of the dead man.

'Seems to me he was reliving his life. Like his mind wouldn't accept he was dying. A lot of it didn't make much sense, but every now and then he'd say something about being made a sheriff when he got back.'

'Got back where?' the undertaker asked.

'No idea,' the doc replied. 'But he did seem to remember his wife, or wives, both killed. The rest became more and more incoherent.'

'Found out who he is yet?' the man asked.

'No, he'll go down as a "John Doe", I guess,' the doc replied. 'At least he has enough money to pay for his own funeral.'

'Long John's what I'll call him,' the undertaker said.

'Long John. That'll do. He's all yours, I got people waiting on me outside.'

William Henry John's body was buried in Flagstone, and the stone cross bears the name 'Long John' to this day.